THE GIRLS OF CANBY HALL

MAKE ME A STAR

EMILY CHASE

SCHOLASTIC INC.
New York Toronto London Auckland Sydney

ISBN 0-590-40440-7

Copyright © 1985 by Mary Lou Kennedy. All rights reserved. Published by Scholastic Inc.

12 11 10 9 8 7 6 5 4 3 2 1   6 7 8 9/8 0/9

THE GIRLS
OF CANBY HALL

MAKE ME
A STAR

THE GIRLS
OF CANBY HALL

Roommates
Our Roommate is Missing
You're No Friend of Mine
Keeping Secrets
Summer Blues
Best Friends Forever
Four is a Crowd
The Big Crush
Boy Trouble
Make Me a Star

CHAPTER ONE

"When you've seen one snowfall, you've seen them all," Dana Morrison said glumly. She gave such an enormous sigh that both of her roommates burst out laughing.

"Dana always takes the weather as a personal affront," Shelley Hyde said with a giggle. She stopped brushing her blonde hair long enough to peer out the dormitory window. It was a dazzlingly bright Saturday morning, and the Canby Hall campus was blanketed in snow. "Why, it's beautiful out there, Dana. A real winter wonderland. What's wrong with you today?"

"I'm just not into soggy mittens and frozen toes," Dana said, unimpressed. "As far as I'm concerned, snow belongs on a ski slope and nowhere else."

"And even then I bet you like to watch it from indoors, curled up in front of a roaring fire, right?" Faith Thompson grinned to take the sting out of the words. She and Shelley

1

Hyde were not only Dana's roommates, but her closest friends, and they liked to tease her about her New York sophistication.

"You're absolutely right," Dana agreed. "I met this fantastic ski instructor once in the Adirondacks —"

"And he taught you how to slalom," Faith said. She grinned and passed Dana a mug of steaming hot chocolate. Cooking was strictly forbidden in Baker House, one of the oldest dorms in Canby Hall, but most of the girls had illegal "hotplates" for tea and cocoa.

"Not quite," Dana said, her lips curling in a smile. "I sprained my ankle on the first day out, so we spent a lot of time sitting side by side —"

"In front of a roaring fire?"

Dana nodded happily. "Looking at his medals." She grinned and tossed her long, brown hair over her shoulder. "It was the best ski trip I ever had."

"We used to make snow angels back home in Iowa," Shelley said wistfully. "And then we'd come inside and Mom would make gallons of snow cream for us."

"Snow cream?" Faith stretched out her long legs and started pulling on a pair of boots. She was sitting on the edge of her mattress, which was on the floor. The girls had stashed their bed frames in storage in September. It was all part of their casual approach to decorating.

The roommates believed that Room 407

was one of the sharpest rooms on campus. The three mattresses were covered with woven spreads and throw pillows, and they looked more like studio couches than beds. Dana's Joffrey Ballet poster dominated one wall, and dozens of black-and-white blow-ups of Faith's photography projects covered another.

"Snow and cream and sugar," Shelley went on. "It's better than ice cream. I bet neither one of you has ever tried it, have you?"

"It must be a Pine Bluff specialty," Dana said. "I've never heard of it in New York."

"It's not a big item in Washington, either," Faith said, as she shrugged into a heavy plaid jacket. "Although come to think of it, I can't imagine big-city snow being the kind you'd like to eat. We're more into building snowmen, I guess. Dad and Richard used to make a giant King Kong every winter."

She felt a peculiar lump rise in her throat whenever she mentioned her father. He was a policeman, and had been shot and killed when he tried to stop a bank robbery. He had left behind a close-knit family, including Faith and her mother; along with Sarah, her older sister; and Richard, her younger brother. Sarah was on full scholarship at Georgetown, and Faith's mother was employed as a social worker. *Life goes on*, Faith thought ruefully, *even though things will never be the same again.*

"Well, you two just don't know what you're

missing," Shelley said feelingly. "Winter wouldn't be winter without snow cream!" Sometimes she really felt like a small-town hick in front of Dana and Faith. Dana was the ultimate New Yorker — bright, articulate, with a mind that raced a mile a minute. Her mother was a buyer for a New York department store and she looked like she had just stepped off a magazine cover.

Shelley looked at Dana and sighed. She was wearing a black T-shirt with a red bandanna around her neck and pencil-slim designer jeans with a chunky silver belt. It took a lot of style, and a skinny waist, to carry off an outfit like that, she thought.

Faith was another city girl, and at first, Shelley hadn't quite known how to take her. Tall and slim with a quick mind and a great sense of humor, she was one of the few black girls at Canby Hall. After an initial "oil and water" period, and a lot of misunderstandings, all three girls in 407 had become great friends.

"You're wrong about all snowflakes looking alike, you know," Faith said to Dana. "In fact, if you two want to brave the elements with me, I'll teach you all about the crystalline structure of snowflakes. No two snowflakes are identical."

"Just what I need, a science lesson," Dana groaned. "And from Nanook of the North," she added with a giggle. "Faith, have you looked at yourself? You look like you're ready to lead a team of sled dogs."

"My aunt knitted this muffler for me," Faith said defensively. No matter how many times she wrapped the muffler around her neck, the ends still trailed her knees.

"She must have thought you were a lot taller," Shelley said innocently.

"Or a giraffe," Dana said, and exploded with laughter.

"That's enough out of you two," Faith said, and tossed a pillow at them. "C'mon, who wants to go outside with me? I've got to take some pictures of the first snowfall of the season. It's for next week's *Clarion*." Faith had landed the job of star reporter on the school newspaper and was always on the lookout for good stories.

"In this weather?" Dana said in alarm. "It's practically a . . . blizzard out there!"

"That's the best way to get pictures of snow," Faith said cheerfully. "Now let's go before everything melts."

Dana and Shelley exchanged a look. "Okay," Dana said finally. "If I weren't bored out of my mind, I'd never do this, but you're on." She turned to Shelley. "How about you?"

"I can't resist the chance to make a snow angel," Shelley said a little sheepishly. "I guess I'm just a small-town girl at heart."

"We like you anyway," Dana said with a

twinkle in her green eyes. "Okay, Faith, we'll shoot snowflakes, if that's what will make you really happy. And then let's visit Alison. Maybe she's heard of this mysterious and wonderful thing called snow cream."

"Are you sure I'm doing this right?" Alison Cavanaugh said hesitantly as she began vigorously stirring the snow cream. "I'm not sure how much sugar I put in."

"It doesn't matter," Shelley assured her. "You can't do it wrong, because there isn't any real recipe. You just taste it as you go along. Paul and I used to make quarts of it." She sighed, remembering the good times she had had with Paul, her one-and-only back in Pine Bluff, Iowa.

"I'll try it," Dana offered. She plunged a spoon into the dish and made a face. "It still tastes like snow," she said, disappointed.

"That's because you need to freeze it, silly." Alison grinned at her, and put the bowl in the freezer. "Let's all have some hot chocolate and you can tell me what you've been up to."

Alison didn't fit anybody's idea of a house-mother, Shelley decided, as they crowded into her comfortable living room. She was young, in her twenties, and loved Indian blouses and handmade jewelry. She had a mass of reddish-brown hair that refused to be tamed, and a slim figure that Shelley envied.

And her apartment on the top floor of Baker was a dream, she thought, admiring the wide, plank floors and hanging baskets of ferns. Alison always called her place "The Penthouse." It had walls of bookcases, and so many windows and skylights, you felt like you were in a treehouse.

"So you've been shooting snowflakes?" she said questioningly to Faith.

"All afternoon," Faith answered. "I think I have enough material for a five-part series," she added with a laugh. Her dark eyes were bright with excitement, and her Afro framed her face in a tangle of curls. "I would have stayed out longer, but Dana started to fade when the sun went down."

"I feel like I've been climbing Mount Everest," Dana said weakly. She was sprawled on a big floor pillow, and reached for a plate of cookies on the coffee table. "I told you I wasn't the outdoors type," she said reproachfully.

"I believe you!" Faith protested. Everyone was silent for a moment, and then Faith added, "How about you, Alison? How did you spend the afternoon?"

"I have to confess, I'm not the outdoors type either," she said. A hint of a blush swept over her cheeks. "I went to a movie in town with Michael."

Faith glanced quickly at Dana, to see how she would react. Just a few short months ago, Dana had had an enormous crush on Michael Frank, the guidance counselor. It had been a sticky situation for everyone concerned, Faith remembered. Especially when Alison and Michael started dating and fell in love. . . .

"That's nice," Dana said warmly. She smiled at Alison, and Faith realized that the crush and the confused feelings were all part of the past.

Everybody chatted for awhile, and then Alison glanced at her watch. "We better sample the snow cream right now, gang, because time's marching on. Before you know it, it will be lights out."

She headed out to the kitchen, and Shelley couldn't resist a smile. *Whether she looks the part or not, she's still a housemother!* she thought.

A few days later, it was time for one of Canby Hall's most hallowed traditions — the Wednesday morning assembly. "It's too early for this," Faith muttered as the three roommates hunted for seats in the assembly hall of Main Building. The room was packed, and there was a low buzz of conversation.

"You're just not a morning person," Dana teased her. "Let's grab those seats in the back row. Then if you doze off, P.A. won't notice." P.A. was an affectionate nickname for Miss Patrice Allardyce, the headmistress.

"Are you kidding?" Faith retorted. "She's got eyes like a hawk. She could spot a field mouse at a hundred yards."

They had just sat down when Pamela Young slid into a seat on the aisle. Pamela was blonde, beautiful, and the daughter of a famous movie star. She was thoroughly disliked by most of the girls at school, and even Shelley had to admit that she wasn't one of her "favorite people." The three roommates had had a big run-in with her once before, and she had almost succeeded in breaking them up. Pamela ran a hand through her thick, blonde hair and sighed theatrically.

"Do you think it's possible to die from boredom?" she said plaintively to no one in particular. "I think I lose a few I.Q. points every time I go to one of these things." She gave a world-weary sigh that Dana found very annoying. *She acts like she should be lounging on a yacht on the Riviera instead of stuck at Canby Hall,* she thought.

Shelley pondered the question. "I've heard of people dying from broken hearts," she said finally, "but not from boredom."

Dana turned to Pamela. "Anyway, I don't think anyone's ever died from Wednesday morning assembly, Pamela."

Sometimes Pamela was just too much to take, Dana decided, turning her attention to the stage. Her mother was Yvonne Young, the movie star, and Pamela never let you forget it for a minute. It was obvious that she felt she was "doing time" at Canby Hall. She enjoyed being an outsider, and made it a point to dress as flamboyantly as possible. On this particular morning, she was wearing a filmy silk blouse and clingy suede pants instead of pastel T-shirts and jeans like the rest of the girls.

Pamela smiled sweetly at Dana and didn't answer, because just then Patrice Allardyce walked to the podium. You could set your watch by her. Every Wednesday morning, at precisely nine o'clock, she held an assembly. Nothing earth-shaking ever happened at these get-togethers, but everyone was expected to be there anyway.

Dana stifled an enormous yawn as Miss Allardyce began to speak. She tuned out the routine announcements about bicycle parking and laundry room etiquette ("It's very inconsiderate to leave your clothes in the dryer overnight. . . .") and let her mind drift to other things. In fact, she was getting ready to indulge in some delicious daydreams, when Miss Allardyce dropped a bombshell.

"I wasn't going to mention this until it was definite," she said, patting her perfect blonde chignon. "But I know how quickly rumors can spread through a boarding school." She paused and stared at the audience. She knew she had everyone's interest. "The fact is, girls, that a movie company has asked my permission to make a film here at Canby Hall."

A ripple of excited questions went through the audience, and she held up her hand for silence. "Girls, please. I said, they asked." She stressed the last word. "I did not say that I agreed." A collective moan went up and she gave a thin smile. "The financial rewards for the school would be considerable, but I have to think the matter over very carefully. I'm not sure how the presence of a movie company would affect your studies. And here at Canby Hall, academic life must come first."

"A little show business would certainly make life more interesting," Casey Flint whispered to Shelley. Casey was a bubbly girl who had become a close friend of the girls in 407. Her love of adventure sometimes got her into sticky situations, but all three girls loved her wacky sense of humor.

"It sure would!" Shelley agreed. Shelley dreamed of becoming an actress, and her pulse raced at the idea of meeting some real live movie stars. Her blue eyes were wide with excitement when she turned to Dana. "Can you imagine — they may make a movie here!" she exclaimed.

"I heard," Dana said calmly. Actually, Dana was excited at the news, too, but was making a tremendous effort to appear nonchalant about the whole thing.

"Please girls, let me continue." Miss Allardyce stood poised and beautiful in a tailored silk suit. She waited until the room was quiet enough to hear a pin drop. "There will be some . . . scouts . . . on campus during the next few days. They'll be looking over the buildings and the grounds, and I've told them to make themselves at home. I think it goes without saying that I will expect each and every one of you to conduct yourself like a Canby Hall girl." She stared pointedly at the girls in the back row, and Dana could have sworn she was looking right at Casey.

She went on with a few more notices, but no one was really listening. Shelley was gripping the armrest so tightly, her knuckles were almost white. "A movie!" she said softly. "I can't believe it."

Casey Flint looked at Faith and said, laughing, "Shelley's gone Hollywood."

"How can you be so calm and cool about it, when it's absolutely the most fantastic thing to ever hit the campus?" Shelley demanded that afternoon at the Tutti-Frutti.

Dana dug into her marshmallow, lemon, and walnut sundae and said quietly, "Because it's not definite, Shelley. Sure, I think it would be fun to have a movie company turn up on campus, but I'm not going to hold my breath."

"I guess it all depends on whether or not Canby Hall is what they're looking for," Faith interjected.

"Well, why wouldn't it be?" Shelley demanded indignantly. "It's the most beautiful campus in the world." She attacked her banana split with renewed energy. "In fact, I think it's the prettiest place I've ever seen. Outside of Iowa, that is."

Dana and Faith looked at each other and smiled. "I'm not sure how much of a recommendation that is," Dana teased her. "But I hope you're right. In fact, maybe you'll even be discovered, and they'll make you a star."

"Do you really think so?" Shelley gulped. She stopped eating, and her spoon was poised in midair.

"It's certainly possible," Dana went on. "A lot of unknowns get their big break that way. That's how one of my sister's friends got a part in a soap."

"Really?" Shelley said.

"Yeah," Dana said thoughtfully. "She and Maggie were at the earring counter in Bloomingdale's when a talent scout spotted her."

Suddenly Shelley stood up and pushed her banana split away. "That does it. I'm starting a diet. As of this minute."

"Shelley, don't be silly. You just ordered that." Faith shot an annoyed look at Dana. Shelley had always been supersensitive about the fact that she was a few pounds overweight.

"Uh, Shelley, I didn't mean you have to starve yourself . . ." Dana began.

Shelley beamed at her. "That's okay, Dana. What's a banana split compared to an acting career? If you're going to be a star, you have to be willing to pay the price." She tossed her jacket over her shoulders. "I'll see you back at the dorm, guys. I want to get my beauty sleep."

When she left, Faith flashed a "now-you've-done-it" look at Dana.

"Don't say it, please, just don't say it." Dana grinned and held up her hand.

"You realize what you've done, don't you?" Faith demanded.

"I know what you're thinking. I've probably created a monster." She paused and smiled. "I wouldn't worry about it too much, though. I've got the sneaky feeling that the movie is never going to come through, anyway."

CHAPTER TWO

Shelley spotted the notice that Friday. It was a small, handwritten card posted conspicuously on the bulletin board in Main Building.

FOXFIRE PRODUCTIONS WILL BEGIN SHOOTING A FEATURE FILM AT CANBY HALL NEXT WEEK. THERE WILL BE NO CHANGE IN CLASS SCHEDULES AND WE ANTICIPATE NO DISRUPTION OF NORMAL SCHOOL ACTIVITIES. PLEASE CONSULT WITH YOUR HOUSEMOTHERS FOR MORE DETAILS. THANK YOU. P. ALLARDYCE.

"I knew it!" Shelley shrieked. She enveloped Faith in an enormous bear hug, and almost swept her off her feet.

"Hey, watch it," Faith protested. "Do you know how much lenses cost nowadays?" She shifted her camera bag over her shoulder and gently disentangled herself.

"What's money? We're all going to be movie stars!"

"So they finally made it official," Pamela

15

Young said quietly. "It's about time." She was wearing a bright pink *Flashdance*-style shirt that left one shoulder almost bare.

Faith caught on first. "You knew about it all along, didn't you? I thought you were being a little too cool about everything."

"I have to admit, I had first-hand information," Pamela said coyly. "It just so happens that my mother is a friend of Tony Albritton, the director —"

Shelley's mouth dropped open, but no words came out. "Your mother . . . is a friend of the director?" she finally said. She hated herself for sounding so impressed, but she couldn't help it. Even though Pamela was a hopeless snob, and impossibly conceited, she was the nearest thing to a celebrity that Shelley had ever met.

Pamela nodded. "They did a year of summer stock together. In fact, she has a small part in the movie they're doing here. You'll get to meet her, Shelley. In person." She grinned when she saw Shelley's stricken expression.

"If I get to meet Yvonne Young, I'll die," Shelley said, shaking her head slowly from side to side. "I'll absolutely die."

"Don't be silly." Pamela gave a little rippling laugh that sounded suspiciously like she had practiced it. "She's really nice. She doesn't act like a movie star at all. Even though she is," she added quickly, for the benefit of some upperclassmen who were passing by. "Look, I'll catch you two later, okay? I'm expecting a call from Yvonne any minute."

"Yvonne?" Casey Flint joined the group just in time to get a withering look from Pamela. "Don't tell me we're getting a double dose of the Young family. I don't know if I can take it," she added when Pamela disappeared down the hall.

Shelley said reproachfully, "I know she's impossible sometimes, but her mother *is* a famous movie star."

"Excuse me while I faint," Casey said, breaking into a wide grin.

"Maybe by some miracle, her mother is nicer than she is," Faith said thoughtfully.

"And maybe she's worse." Casey shrugged. She just wasn't impressed by Pamela, the way Shelley was. Casey's parents were famous art dealers in New York, and she had grown up among rich and successful people. Unlike Pamela, though, she never bragged about her famous friends, and played down her background. She liked bargain basement clothes, and her favorite outfit was a pair of faded jeans and a T-shirt.

"What do you say we visit Alison after dinner, and find out what this movie deal is all about," Casey suggested. "She's bound to have some inside information."

"Yeah, that's a great idea," Shelley said. "Come by the room around seven, and we'll all see Alison together." She glanced at her watch. "If I can manage to stay alive till then," she added with a dramatic sigh. "I'm so excited, my heart's beating like a rabbit's."

"You'll live," Faith said flatly. "I know just the thing to calm you down. How about a nice long drill on French verbs? Everything from the pluperfect to the subjunctive. How does that sound?"

"Like slow torture," Shelley groaned. French had always been her weak point, and Faith had had to bail her out more than once.

"C'mon, mon amie," Faith said, tossing an arm around her shoulders. "The hours will whiz by, and before you know it, the magic hour of seven will be here."

When they knocked on Alison's door later that night, they heard an excited buzz of voices from inside. "I think a few of the kids beat us to it," Casey said.

Alison opened the door. "Welcome to Cavanaugh's Casting Agency," she said wryly. They filed in, and saw that at least half of Baker Hall was already sprawled on the floor. "Hey, keep it down," Alison pleaded. "There are a few kids left in the dorm who are trying to study."

"How can they study at a time like this?" Shelley said wonderingly.

Alison smiled. "Not everyone's as thrilled at the movie business as you are." She lowered her voice. "I think Miss Allardyce is having second thoughts about the whole thing. In fact, if she saw the crowd in here tonight, she'd be having third and fourth thoughts." She stepped over a bag of potato chips and said, "It's time to get things moving."

She rapped a pencil against a glass. "I think everybody's here for the same reason," she said, smiling.

"We all need help with our math homework," Casey said with a straight face.

"I wish it was that simple," Alison countered. "Okay, let me try to tell you what I know about the movie, and then you can ask questions. But not too many questions," she added swiftly, "because this is a school night, after all." She paused, and ran a hand through her reddish-brown hair. "Oh, I'm just no good at making speeches," she said apologetically. "Let's start over. You can ask me what you want to know." She lowered herself onto a bean bag chair and opened a can of Tab.

"What's the name of the movie?" Shelley said breathlessly.

Alison grinned. "That I do know. It's called *Midnight Whispers*."

"I love it!" Dana said. "Is it a horror flick?"

"It certainly is," Alison said. "I haven't read the script, but Miss Allardyce has. She says it's about a spirit that haunts a girls' school."

"An evil spirit," someone spoke up. Dana glanced around the room to see who it was, and spotted Pamela.

"I should have known Pamela would get

her two cents in," she whispered to Faith. "She always has to steal the show." Pamela was perched on the window bench, in her best designer jeans and a black fishnet top. She looked every inch the daughter of a famous movie star.

"Is it true that your mother is in the movie?" a freshman asked, and everybody stared at Pamela.

"Yes," she said smugly. "She plays Marion Reed, the housemother. I'd tell you more, but I'm not allowed to give away the plot."

"You'd think she was talking about giving away atomic secrets," Faith said in a low voice to Dana.

There was a moment of silence while everyone absorbed this information, and then Alison took the floor again. "Uh, I think the main thing that Miss Allardyce would like me to stress, is that classes will go on as usual."

"Okay, now that you've said that, tell us the interesting stuff," Casey prompted.

That got a laugh, and Alison said, "Just ask me."

Faith spoke up. "When does the cast arrive and where are they staying? I want to get some pictures for the *Clarion*."

"Next week. The main actors will have their own trailers, and the minor characters and extras will be staying in Greenleaf." Greenleaf, Massachusetts, was a small town just a mile from the campus. Alison frowned. "Talk to me later about the pictures, though,

Faith. There was some question about whether or not picture-taking would be allowed."

"What! I can't do a feature article without pictures," she complained.

"Speaking of extras," Shelley said a little nervously, "will we able to audition for parts?"

This was obviously the question that everybody was waiting for. Alison hesitated. "The answer is yes . . . but with restrictions."

"Yes, but with restrictions? What does that mean?" a pretty freshman asked. It was obvious that she wanted to land a movie role.

"Don't hate me for suggesting it," Alison teased, "but the restrictions are that your studies must come first. In other words, you may not skip class to audition, or to watch any of the shooting, or to do a walk-on part. And that's not my rule. It comes straight from the top. From Miss Allardyce."

"But we can try? We'll really get a shot at being in the movie?" the girl persisted.

"Sure. As far as I know, they'll be casting a few extras, and maybe even a few minor roles here. They promised to hold open auditions, so if you've got the talent, and the time, you've got my blessing. Like they say, go for it."

"I will. Oh, I will," Shelley said softly. Faith and Dana exchanged looks, but Shelley was too starry-eyed to notice.

At eight o'clock, Alison shooed everyone out the door. "Remember, studies first, everybody. Hollywood can wait, but math tests are here and now."

"You had to say that," Casey muttered. She turned to Dana. "Are you going to audition?"

"Oh, I'll go to watch," Dana said lightly. "And I want to protect my roomie, here," she said, nodding to Shelley.

"Hey, I don't need protection," Shelley said indignantly. "I may just steal a great part out from under all your noses."

"Yeah, Shelley's gonna play the evil spirit," Casey teased.

"Actually, the spirit is a very good part, because she's on screen for about half the movie," Pamela said crisply. "In fact, that part has already been cast in L.A."

Shelley was impressed. "You know all the trade secrets, don't you?"

"I know a few things," Pamela said sweetly. "I could probably give you a few tips on auditioning, if you're interested. You know you've only got three minutes to impress the casting director."

"I do?" Shelley tried not to let any excitement creep into her voice, but it was hopeless. She even reminded herself that Pamela was a rat who once had tried to break up the friendship of the girls in 407, and nearly succeeded. It didn't help. Once Pamela started talking about movies, she was hooked. All over again.

"At the most," Pamela added firmly. She drew Shelley to one side as the rest of the girls headed back to the fourth floor. "In fact, I might be able to snitch one of the scripts for us to look at. Then you'd have a big jump on everyone else at the auditions."

Shelley hesitated. She didn't want to be disloyal to her friends, but this was the chance of a lifetime. "That would be fantastic!" she blurted out.

"But just keep it between us, okay? I don't want to cause any hard feelings."

"Oh sure, I understand," Shelley said. She practically floated back to her room. Not only was she going to audition for a movie, but she was going to be coached by a pro! This would surely be her big break. She just knew it!

The girls in 407 were too restless to sleep that night, and each was alone with her thoughts.

Dana pulled the covers up to her chin and stared at the shaft of moonlight that filtered in the dorm window. *I hope Shelley doesn't get too caught up in this movie,* she thought worriedly. She remembered what had happened when Shelley landed a part in a school play. She had gotten so involved with the production — and with the male lead — that she had neglected everything else. Her grades had plummeted to an all-time low, and she had almost flunked out of Canby Hall. *I'll have to keep an eye out for her this time,* Dana decided. *It's obvious she's been bitten by the acting bug. Again.*

Faith gave the pillow a vigorous thump and tried to make her mind a blank. *I've got to get some sleep so I can be fresh for tomorrow,* she repeated over and over. The trouble was, it was hard to sleep when she thought about doing a feature on the movie. It could be the biggest story of her career! How often do reporters get to cover something like this? *I need just the right lead,* she decided. Maybe something like "Lights! Cameras! Action!" or "There's no business like show business." Something really cute, and catchy. . . .

Shelley felt as wide awake as if it were morning. A movie! Right here at Canby Hall! It felt like Christmas and Easter and her birthday all rolled into one. It was the best surprise of her life, and she still couldn't believe it was happening to her. *And I won't be nervous at the audition,* she told herself. *Pamela will help me, and she's been through this a million times before . . . this is my one chance to be an actress, and I'm not going to bungle it!*

CHAPTER THREE

The movie was definitely the hottest topic of conversation to hit the Canby Hall campus. Dana was playing it supercool the following night, even though everybody else at Pizza Pete's was asking a million questions.

"Well, what did Pamela say exactly?" a girl from Addison House asked her. "Is her mother really flying in from Hollywood?"

"I guess so," Dana said. "She's got a part in the movie. In fact, she plays a housemother."

"Yvonne Young, a housemother. I can't believe it!" the girl squealed. "Well, I guess I better get back to my date," she said reluctantly. "If you hear anything else, let me know."

"I will," Dana promised. As soon as the girl left, she turned to her boyfriend, Randy Crowell. "I bet you're sick of all this."

"A little," he admitted, and passed her

another piece of pizza. "But I've got the feeling it's going to get worse once the movie company gets here, right, Johnny?" He grinned at Johnny Bates, Faith's boyfriend.

"I can guarantee it," Johnny answered. "I don't think Canby Hall or Greenleaf will ever be the same." He sighed. "They're already selling bumper stickers saying, "Greenleaf — home of *Midnight Whispers*."

"Well, at least it put your town on the map," Faith teased him. Both the boys were from Greenleaf. Johnny Bates went to the local high school, and Randy Crowell came from a prominent family of big landowners.

"They even called Dad about doing some location shooting out on the ranch," Randy said.

"Really?" Dana looked at him in surprise. "That would be fun. Did he say yes?"

"No way," Randy said flatly. "All those trucks and people would really spook the horses."

"I never thought of that," Dana admitted.

"You city types never do," Randy told her with a smile. He had finished high school in Greenleaf, but had decided not to head for college right away. He worked hard on his family's horse ranch, and loved every minute of it.

"You're slowly educating me," Dana told him drily. It was true. She and Randy were complete opposites in many ways — she liked the Stones and he liked Willie Nelson — but

they had a lot to offer each other. She had
taught him about poetry, and he had taught
her how to identify wild flowers. They were
friends, more than anything else, and it was
a nice relationship to have, she decided. Their
friendship had almost ended earlier that year
when Shelley and Randy had started dating
for a short time, but Dana and Randy had
weathered that storm and become even better
friends than before.

"I think Faith plans to make her fame and
fortune off *Midnight Whispers*," Johnny said.

"Not as an actress," Faith said in response
to Randy's puzzled look. "I'm looking at it as
a photo opportunity — the chance to put together a really dynamite portfolio."

"I think you'll do a terrific job," Johnny
said proudly. He smiled at her, and pre-
dictably, she felt herself go weak in the knees.

"I hope so," she said softly. "It's a once in
a lifetime chance."

Nobody said anything for a moment, and
then Randy cleared his throat. "Uh, unless
anyone wants to order another pizza. . . ."

"No, let's split, man," Johnny agreed
quickly. It was getting late and it would soon
be curfew time for the girls.

"I'd offer you a ride, but I've got the
pick-up truck," Randy said apologetically.
"It's a two-seater."

Johnny grinned at him. "That's okay. It's
only a mile back to Canby Hall."

"But it's cold out," Dana said. "Are you sure you won't freeze on the way?"

"We'll just have to stick very close together," Johnny said with a grin.

"Or we could walk fast," Faith said practically.

Johnny rolled his eyes. "Party-pooper."

When Randy pulled up in front of Baker House, he kept the engine running. "C'mere," he said softly to Dana. She slid close to him, and he wrapped his arms around her. "That's better," he said. "I wanted to kiss you all night."

"You did?" she said, nuzzling against him.

"I did." He bent down and kissed her very gently. "But it was hard with a giant pepperoni pizza between us."

She laughed. "Where there's a will, there's a way." She smiled at him. He was really remarkably good-looking, she thought. His steely gray eyes looked deep and mysterious in the dark truck, and she loved the way his blond hair curled over his collar.

"Am I going to lose you for the duration of the movie?" he asked her.

"Of course not," she said indignantly. "Shelley's the movie nut, not me. I'm not even going to try out for anything." She rested her cheek on his rough sheepskin jacket. "As far as I'm concerned, *Midnight Whispers* doesn't even exist." She paused, and then laughed. "Although come to think of it,

Shelley will probably remind me of it. Twenty-four hours a day. She's going to be absolute murder to live with!"

"Well, the sooner they get here, the sooner it'll be over with," Randy said huskily. "And then everything will be back to normal." He bent his head down close to hers. "But let's not worry about the movie anymore, okay? I've got exactly three minutes left to kiss you."

The next few days flew by, and Dana didn't think much about the movie at all. At least not until the following Wednesday morning, when Shelley blasted everyone out of bed.

"They're here!" Shelley yelled. She clutched her pink quilted robe tightly around her, and hopped up and down on one foot. "Oh, this floor is like ice," she complained. "I don't think the heat makes it up to the fourth floor."

"Put on some slippers and pipe down," came a muffled voice from Faith's bed. "Some of us are trying to sleep."

"I don't want to leave the window. I might miss something," Shelley answered.

"What's all the commotion about?" Dana sat up in bed, blinking groggily like she had just come out of a trance. Her long, brown hair tumbled around her shoulders, and she gave an enormous yawn.

"They're here," Shelley repeated. Her eyes were riveted to the main quadrangle.

Dana started to get out of bed, then changed her mind and burrowed back under the covers. She was wearing a Gilley's T-shirt, instead of her usual pajamas, and her feet were like blocks of ice. "Who's here? Honestly, Shelley, you'd think the Martians had landed." She peered at the bedside clock and groaned. "It's six-fifteen."

"It's much more exciting than Martians. It's the movie crew."

"Why didn't you say so?" Dana leaped out of bed and nearly collided with Faith who was dashing to the window. They both stared blankly out at the parking lot.

"That's it?" Faith said, disappointed. "Some movie crew. It looks like a Good Humor truck."

"Well, it's a start," Shelley said defensively. She peered at a white truck with Foxfire Productions stenciled in black letters on the side. "Look, someone's getting out!"

"Get your camera, Faith," Dana said sarcastically. "Maybe it's Rick Springfield."

They watched as two young men in jeans started setting up camera equipment. They had trouble getting the tripod to stand up on the icy walk and after several unsuccessful attempts, they got back in the truck and drove off.

"I wonder what that was all about?" Shelley looked crushed. "Do you think they'll be back?"

"I'm sure of it," Faith said. "In fact, I bet

by lunchtime this place will be crawling with real live movie stars." She started to go back to bed but stopped when the alarm went off. "But in the meantime, we have classes to go to, remember? Like Alison said, movies come and go, but math tests are here to stay." She paused. "And didn't you say you had a French quiz today, mademoiselle?"

Shelley jumped like she had been shot. "On the subjunctive! I'm doomed."

"Honestly, Shelley," Dana said. "Don't you want to do well?"

"Of course I do," Shelley said, yanking open her French book. "It's just that —"

"You'd rather be in pictures," Dana finished for her. She stomped out of the room, exasperated, and Shelley sighed. *Sometimes your best friends don't understand you at all,* she thought. *In fact, there are probably only two people in the whole world who understand how much this movie means to me.* Tom Stevenson, her boyfriend, would definitely understand. He wanted to be an actor himself. And the other person, as crazy as it sounded, was Pamela Young. She loved the movie business, too.

Shelley shrugged and went back to her French book. She only had fifteen minutes to learn all about the past perfect tense, but she was having a terrible time concentrating. How could anybody expect her to worry about French verbs on a day like this? She glanced at her watch. Did she dare cut class?

No, she decided, she'd better not. Her grades weren't that great to start with. *Just hang in there till this afternoon,* she told herself. *The movie company will still be here.*

When Shelley came out of class at three o'clock, she couldn't believe her eyes. Faith's prediction had come true. Canby Hall looked exactly like a backlot for Universal Studios. There were dozens of people milling around the campus, plus a collection of trucks, cars, and trailers. Everybody was moving quickly, purposefully, as if they didn't have a minute to waste. She and Dana moved just in time as a shiny white truck backed over one of Miss Allardyce's prize rosebushes.

"Sorry, girls," the driver said cheerfully. He stuck his head out the window and grinned at them, and then gunned the engine and left them in a cloud of dust.

"What do you suppose they're doing?" Shelley breathed softly. She flinched when she heard the grinding noise of a chain saw. A boy in a parka and jeans had shimmied up one of the stately elms, and was busily cutting down branches.

"It beats me," Dana answered. "P.A. is going to have a fit when she sees what they've done to the campus, though. You know how fussy she is."

Equipment was strewn everywhere, and the general impression was one of mass confusion.

A girl with a megaphone was begging for "anyone from Wardrobe" to go to the production office, but no one was paying any attention to her. She glanced hopefully at Dana and Shelley, and then continued forlornly down the main walkway.

Dana and Shelley walked slowly past the dining hall and the science building, taking it all in. When they got to the library, they were surprised to see three tents set up outside. Two were marked "Wardrobe," and the third had a hand-lettered sign that said "Makeup."

"Excuse me," a girl with frizzy red hair said brusquely. She was carrying two big tote bags, and nearly pushed Dana off the sidewalk. "Are you here to be made up?"

"Oh, no," Dana started to explain. "We're just watching. . . ."

"Well, would you mind moving on? You're holding up the line."

Dana glanced behind her. "I didn't even know there was a line," she muttered softly.

"Do you think she's anyone famous?" Shelley asked in an awestruck tone.

"Shelley, she does makeup. Couldn't you figure that out?"

"Well you don't have to snap at me," Shelley said plaintively. "I can't figure out who's who around here."

It was hard to tell who was in the cast, and who was in the crew, Dana admitted. All the technicians looked like actors, as they strutted around the campus in jeans and heavy parkas and cowboy boots.

"Aren't they gorgeous?" Shelley whispered. "They all look like they belong on *Dallas*."

"Better than Paul?" Dana said mischievously. Paul had been Shelley's steady back home in Iowa, before Shelley decided she wasn't ready to settle down with one boy.

"Well," Shelley said hesitantly, "not better, just different."

"You're certainly loyal." Dana paused to flash a big smile at a young man carrying a sound boom. "I've seen some guys here today that could make me forget Bret Harper ever existed." She laughed. "And there was a time when I thought he was the only boy in the world for me. It's funny how things change, isn't it?"

"It sure is." They crossed the edge of campus, and headed toward Greenleaf. They were going to the Tutti-Frutti, a favorite hangout, to meet Casey and Faith. Instead of taking their usual shortcut by the wishing pond, they were taking the long way around to "check out the scenery," as Dana said. So far, they had seen a lot of cables and cameras, but no stars.

"It's funny, isn't it?" Shelley said. "When I first came here, all I wanted to do was get back to Iowa as quickly as I could. I figured my whole life was there — my school, my family, and of course, Paul. But Canby Hall changed all that. Now I know what I want more than anything in the world. I want to be an actress."

Dana stared at her. "Shelley —"

"Oh, I know. You probably think I'm crazy." She gave a little laugh. "You think that deep down, I'm still a real farm girl. But you're wrong, honest. I'm going to be a star someday. You just wait and see."

"I don't think you're crazy," Dana said quietly. "I just hope you know what you're going after. And I hope you get it."

"Oh, I will, Dana. Don't you worry. And I know just where to start."

CHAPTER FOUR

"Did anybody see anyone famous?" Shelley demanded a few minutes later at the Tutti-Frutti. Casey and Faith had grabbed a corner table and were working their way through chocolate-marshmallow sundaes.

"It's hard to say. The guys all look terrific to me," Casey said with a grin.

"I know what you mean," Dana agreed. "We had the same problem. Remember that dreamy-looking guy in the suede vest, Shelley? I was convinced he was the star, and then he threw about fifty feet of cable over his shoulder and climbed a pole."

"I still haven't gotten any shots for my story," Faith said resignedly. "First Alison has to check with Miss Allardyce, and then I have to get written permission from the production manager. I suppose there's no hurry, because most of the actors aren't arriving till next week."

"Has anybody heard anything about auditions?" a ponytailed junior yelled from a neighboring table. "I've been asking around, but no one seems to know anything."

Faith shook her head. "All I know is that Miss Allardyce said that everything will be posted on that big bulletin board in the cafeteria. I guess you could check it tonight at dinner."

"I'll check it right now," the girl said, standing up. "Besides," she added with a smile, "it will give me an excuse to take another walk across campus." She tossed her tawny blonde hair over her shoulder and wrapped a bright red muffler around her neck. "Bye, everybody." She flashed a toothpaste smile and posed for a minute by the door. She knew she looked sensational.

"She's sure not wasting any time," Shelley said, annoyed. She felt strangely irritated, and wasn't even sure why. "Look at that! She actually left half her cheeseburger. You'd think it was a matter of life and death."

Faith stared at her in surprise. "What's bugging you, Shelley?"

"Nothing's bugging me," Shelley snapped. Except that wasn't completely true. The problem was that she was beginning to look at everyone as competition. She was jealous, and it surprised her. "I guess I just think that people are making too big a deal over these auditions," she said, trying to save face.

"I've noticed," Dana said wryly.

"What's that supposed to mean?" Shelley demanded.

"Whatever you want it to mean," Dana shrugged.

"Hey, why doesn't everybody settle down and order?" Casey suggested. "The place is going to fill up in a few minutes."

"That's okay, someone can have my seat," Shelley said, jumping up suddenly. "I don't feel very hungry after all." She glared at Dana and picked up her books. "See you later," she said curtly.

Casey stared at Dana in amazement. "What got into her?"

"Acting fever," Dana replied.

Faith said, "Let's hope it's not catching."

Dana saw the notice the very next day. The three roommates were on their way in to dinner at the cafeteria, when Dana said teasingly, "Doesn't anyone want to check the bulletin board with me?" They crowded around the big corkboard, and there it was.

MIDNIGHT WHISPERS. OPEN CALL. EXTRAS, STAND-INS, WALK-ONS. REPORT TO ROOM 101 ADMN. BLDG. 7:00 PM FRIDAY.

"I don't know if I should mention this or not," Dana said with a grin. "But isn't this what you've been waiting for, Shel?"

"That's it," Shelley said softly. She swallowed hard. "Friday. That only gives me two days to get ready."

"How can you get ready for an audition?" Casey laughed. "All you have to do is show up on Friday. If they want you, they'll use you, and —" Shelley stopped her with a look and she flushed. "I just think you're making too big a deal of this," Casey said finally.

"That's your opinion," Shelley said breezily. "You might be in for a big surprise if you decided to audition."

"Oh, I'm going to audition all right," Casey said, her temper flaring. "But I'm not going to make an idiot of myself over this thing."

She stalked away and Shelley looked innocently at Dana and Faith. "Isn't it funny how something like a movie can bring out the worst in people?" Suddenly she saw a familiar figure striding down the aisle, and brightened. Pamela. "I'll see you after dinner, okay? I've got to talk to someone." She hurried off without waiting for a reply.

"Of course," Faith said pointedly. "First things first." It was obvious that Shelley was going to put the movie ahead of everything, she thought disgustedly. Certainly ahead of their friendship!

"Do you really think I'll do okay?" Shelley struggled with her tuna salad, and finally gave up and pushed it away. She wondered how Pamela could be so calm. Her own stomach was growling like a cement mixer, but she was too excited to eat.

"You've asked me a dozen times," Pamela said patiently, "and yes, I'm sure you'll do okay. Better than okay. You'll be terrific."

"Well, I don't know about that," Shelley said modestly. She was secretly pleased that Pamela had so much faith in her. "Did you manage to get the script?"

"No, my mother's shooting a commercial on the West Coast, and I couldn't get a hold of her. But I did find out one interesting bit of news from the A.D."

"A.D.?"

"Assistant Director." She paused and toyed with her omelette. "They're casting more than just extras and stand-ins. They're definitely going to cast a couple of small parts here."

"Really?" Shelley could hardly contain herself. "You mean speaking parts?"

Pamela nodded. "Not a lot of lines, of course," she said airily, "but good parts. You know, even if you have a tiny speaking part, it looks great on your credits."

"I know. It would be fantastic," Shelley said. She sipped her iced tea and tried to calm down. A speaking part! It was more than she had ever dreamed of.

"And you also qualify for membership in S.A.G.," Pamela went on.

"S.A.G. I've heard of that. It's the Screen Actors Guild," Shelley said in a breathless voice.

Pamela gave her a tolerant smile. "Just

think. You'd belong to the same union as Matt Dillon."

"It's hard to believe," Shelley said. Out of the corner of her eye, she saw Dana and Faith staring at her. She wondered what they were thinking. *This is more important than anything,* she told herself. *I can get more tips from Pamela than I could pick up in a year of acting school.* She turned her attention back to Pamela.

"It's up to you, Shelley," Pamela was saying very softly. "All you have to do is get a part. After that, everything will just fall in your lap." She smiled mysteriously. "And I'm going to tell you how to do it."

Shelley smiled back. Pamela had been really rotten in the past, but it looked like she had finally put all her lies and tricks aside. She was really going to help her!

When Shelley got back to Baker House, she found her boyfriend, Tom, waiting for her in the lounge. "Did we have a date?" she blurted out. Her mind was still on the movie, and all the exciting things Pamela had told her.

He grinned at her. "Hey, what kind of a greeting is that? No, we didn't have a date, but there's a million stars out tonight, and I thought we could take a quick walk around the campus."

Shelley hesitated. "I have to do some French homework," she faltered. He looked at her and she smiled. "But come to think of it, you're more fun than the subjunctive tense any day. Let's go."

"Thanks a lot!" he said drily, steering her towards the door.

A few minutes later, they were walking down by the maple grove and Shelley wondered how she could gently tell him that she wouldn't be able to spend much time with him in the coming weeks.

"You mean, we can't even go out on Friday night? It's the one night that I can get the car." He looked so disappointed that Shelley felt like putting her arms around him. "I came out in this subzero weather just to ask you," he said in a hurt tone.

"Tom, didn't you hear a word I said? They're making a movie here. A movie. Read my lips," she teased him. "And I think I'm going to get a part. In fact, you could say it's a sure thing." She was going to tell him that Pamela had promised to help her, and stopped just in time. Tom had always been suspicious of Pamela, and had called her a troublemaker right from the start.

"Well, you won't be tied up all night, will you?" He put his arm around her shoulders as they hurried past the main building. The wind was biting cold as it whipped around her legs.

Shelley sighed. It was going to be hard to make him understand. She had figured that since he wanted to be an actor himself, there wouldn't be any problem. "Maybe not. But I have to keep the evening open, just in case. They could keep us waiting for a long time, and auditions could go on for hours. There's just no way to predict those things. Try to understand, okay?"

"I'll try, but it's going to be hard." He pretended to be thinking. "Maybe you can make it up to me," he said with a grin.

"How could I do that?" she said teasingly.

"I'm sure I'll think of something." They were back at Baker House, and it was almost time for Shelley to get inside or she'd miss curfew. "You know, a couple of kisses just might tide me over until I see you again," he told her.

She stared at him, and pretended to be shocked. "Tom! You know that kissing isn't allowed on campus." She started to smile as they walked up the steps to the front porch.

"I thought I remembered hearing that that rule got broken a lot." He put his arms around her waist and looked down at her.

Shelley quickly slid her arms around his neck, and hoped that it was too cold for anyone else to be out walking.

"Where would you hear a thing like that?" she said softly. She looked up at him, and felt a rush of affection for him. He was really a terrific guy! He was completely different from Paul, her boyfriend back home, but he was very special, just the same.

He kissed her and then drew back and

looked at her very seriously. "Just don't fall for any movie stars, okay?"

"I'll try not to," she teased him. "At least not between now and Saturday."

By Friday, the cast had arrived in full force, and there were more lights and cables strewn everywhere. A central office was set up in an empty classroom in the main building, and a bank of telephones was installed.

"What do you suppose they do in there?" Faith whispered to Shelley. They had walked by the open doorway three times, trying to spot someone famous.

"Pamela said that the actors stop by every morning to find out what scenes they're doing that day. I think they post them on that board over there." Shelley kept her voice low. "And they come in to get their messages, too." She moved to one side to let a pretty young girl pass by.

"Have you seen Jerry around?" the girl said suddenly. Her auburn hair was cut very short, close to her head, and Shelley thought she was one of the most beautiful girls she had ever seen.

"Jerry?" Faith said blankly.

"Jerry in Makeup," the girl went on. "He said he'd be back by twelve to do my eyes. No one else can do them the way he does." She stopped and stared at them. "You're with the film, aren't you?"

"No, I'm afraid we're not," Faith said good-naturedly. "We're just students."

"Oh, sorry. I thought you were in the sorority scene."

"The sorority scene?" Shelley finally managed to find her voice.

The girl laughed. "Yeah, the one where the spirit comes in just when they're cutting the cake, and — oops, I see Jerry," she said suddenly. "It's been fun talking to you. Bye!" She flashed a smile and took off at a run down the hall.

"She thought we were with the movie company," Shelley said, impressed. "We must look like actresses." She tried to sound noncommittal, but she was so thrilled, she felt like jumping up and down.

"Don't get your hopes up," Faith said. "It doesn't mean anything, Shelley. We're the right age for the parts, that's all."

"Oh, I hadn't thought of that," Shelley admitted. Then she smiled. "Well, I'm going to take it as a good omen anyway. Tonight's the audition, you know."

"As if I could forget," Faith muttered under her breath. Shelley had been talking about it nonstop for forty-eight hours!

CHAPTER FIVE

I'll never get used to auditions!" Shelley wailed. "Would you believe it? My knees are shaking." Her mouth was so dry, she could barely get her tongue around the words. The moment she had been alternately dreading and longing for had finally arrived — the Friday night auditions for *Midnight Whispers*.

"Nobody likes auditions," Pamela said airily. "At least that's what Yvonne says. Of course," she couldn't resist adding, "she's beyond the audition stage herself." She took out her compact and checked her eye makeup. "Nobody asks her to read for them anymore. They just tell her what the part is like, and she decides if she wants it or not."

"It must be wonderful," Shelley said quietly.

"Well, it's taken her a long time to get to this point," Pamela admitted. "In the beginning, she had to make the rounds like everybody else, and get a lot of rejections. You've got to have a thick skin in this business, you know."

"Oh, I know. And I do," Shelley said, in a quavery voice. Pamela peered at her suspiciously, and she added, "I'm just a little nervous tonight, that's all."

"A little nervous!" Faith whispered to Dana. "If she wrings her hands anymore, she's going to rub off the top layer of skin."

"She's not the only one," Dana said. "Just take a look around. The tension in here is so thick, you could cut it with a knife."

Faith nodded, and wished for the dozenth time that she had permission to take some pictures. The hall in the main building was crammed with "hopefuls" — girls from every class and every dorm who wanted a part in the movie. Most of them were sitting on the floor, and a few were lounging against the wall, trying to look unconcerned. There was a low buzz of conversation, and some kids had brought Walkmans. It would make an interesting project for her portfolio, she decided. She turned her attention back to Dana. "I just hope she doesn't blow it," she said softly.

"Me, too," Dana whispered back. "I wish this didn't mean so much to her, but apparently it does." Even though her feelings were a little hurt after the scene at the Tutti-Frutti, she wanted Shelley to do well tonight.

"How many do we have out here?" A woman dressed in a yellow silk blouse and beautifully tailored jeans stuck her head around the corner. "Can I count heads, or are some of you just here to watch?"

"Uh, there's five of us auditioning in this group," Pamela volunteered.

"Make that four," Dana amended. "I'm just along for the ride," she explained to the woman.

"Make it three," Faith said. "I'm with the press." She grinned and tapped her notebook.

"Okay, I'm going to get your names, and I promise we'll get to you just as soon as we can," the woman said. "We're going to ask you to come in one at a time to Room 101." She smiled. "By the way, my name's Carol Gate, and I'm the assistant casting director." She moved around the room with a clipboard, and by the time she got to Shelley, Shelley could barely remember her own name.

"Hyde. Shelley Hyde." She stumbled as if it were a foreign language. She picked a non-existent piece of lint off her sweater and took a deep breath. She had changed her clothes three times and had finally settled on tan wool slacks and a pale blue turtleneck.

Things moved quickly after that. Girls were ushered in and out of Room 101 so fast, they barely had time to catch their breath.

"It's like a revolving door," Shelley said worriedly. "And nobody looks too thrilled when they come out."

"You're right. And I can't even get anyone to give me a quote for the *Clarion*," Faith complained. "Before they go in, they're too nervous to talk, and when they come out, they look like a bomb dropped on them."

"I told you," Pamela said darkly. "You've only got three minutes to make an impression on the casting people. They're tough and they don't like to waste time. They can tell right away whether or not they want you." She paused and added a touch of lip gloss to her already perfect makeup. "Remember, they call these things 'cattle calls.' They herd you in like sheep, and then bingo. You've got a part, or you're out the door."

Shelley looked subdued. "I know," she said, letting her breath out slowly.

"Just do what I told you. Speak up and don't keep your nose buried in your script. Don't be afraid to look at the other actors. There's really no big secret to acting." Pamela sighed and managed to look supremely bored.

"Shelley Hyde?" a young man said abruptly.

"Present," Shelley said, and automatically raised her hand. A few girls laughed, and she blushed. "I mean, here I am."

"You're next," he said, and walked away while Shelley scrambled to her feet.

"What do I have to do?" she said, practically running to keep up with him.

"They'll tell you in there," he said without raising his eyes from his notebook. They were standing in front of Room 101. As far as Shelley was concerned, there was a firing squad inside waiting for her. "You'll probably read a few lines for them, or maybe just improvise. Here you go," he said. He nudged her towards the classroom door, which was guarded by a young woman in aviator glasses.

"Hyde," he confirmed, and the girl scratched something off a list.

Shelley's mind was whirling. *Improvise!* That had never been her strong point in acting class. Even Andre Rosofsky, the drama teacher who had directed the summer intensive, had admitted it. "You seem to do much better with a script," he had told her. "You must learn to improvise, because some directors prefer it. But don't worry, Shelley," he had said kindly. "It will come in time."

But I'm out of time, she thought miserably as she found herself facing three unsmiling faces.

"Come in, come in," a woman in a stylish suit said. She was sitting behind a long table with Carol Gate and a man in a heavy white sweater.

Shelley closed the door and walked timidly up to the table. She wondered if she should shake hands or something, but no one bothered making any introductions.

"Pick up one of those sheets and read the part of Hilda," the woman ordered. "From the top."

Hilda . . . it sounds like an important charracter, maybe even a leading part, Shelley thought excitedly. She had no way of knowing. Her hands were trembling and she accidentally knocked the whole sheet of papers to the floor. She heard someone give an exasperated sigh as she bent to pick them up.

"I'll get them," Carol said quickly. "You just read, Shelley."

Shelley slowly got up and stared at the paper. She had never had to do a "cold reading" before, but Mr. Rosofsky had warned her about them. "Directors like to see if actors can think on their feet, Shelley. But be careful. Cold readings are murder for the actors. You only have a few seconds to figure out what the character is about and then try to project it." The trouble was, she knew nothing about Hilda, and had absolutely no idea where to start!

"We need to begin," the woman in the suit snapped.

Shelley took a deep breath and plunged in. "It's a beautiful night, isn't it, Eddie?" She didn't have a clue who Eddie was, or why they were out together.

"Yeah, there must be a million stars out." To her surprise, the man in the sweater was reading Eddie's lines. He didn't sound at all like an actor, though, and he read them in a flat monotone. By the time Shelley recovered, it was her turn again. "I've always loved it down here by the lake. It's my favorite place on campus."

She started to turn the page, when the woman in the suit stopped her with a curt, "That's enough. Thank you very much."

"That's it?" Shelley blurted out. How could it be over? She had only read a few lines. She hadn't had a chance to show them what she could do!

Carol shrugged. "You'll be hearing from us."

She stumbled out the door and practically ran into Faith and Casey. She had made a mess of everything. She just knew it!

"How was it, Shelley?" Faith asked. She tried to give Shelley an encouraging smile, but the look on Shelley's face said it all.

"You don't want to know," Shelley insisted, shaking her head.

Casey laughed to lighten things up. "Oh, hey, it can't be as bad as all that."

"It's worse," Shelley breathed softly. "Believe me." She stared at her friends for a moment, and then turned and slowly made her way toward the front door.

"Shouldn't we go with her?" Dana said.

"She'll be fine," Pamela said quickly. "Besides, Casey and I still have to audition."

Suddenly Casey turned pale. "They're calling my name. Wish me luck!"

"No, wait. That's the worst thing to do," Pamela purred. "You're supposed to say break a leg."

"Then break a leg," Faith said fervently. She turned to Dana. "You're sure you don't want to change your mind and audition?"

Dana laughed. "Are you kidding? After looking at Shelley? I think I'd have much more fun at a chemistry final."

"Then, if you don't mind, I'm going to go after Shelley. I'll give her a few minutes to get back to the room, and cry or throw pillows, or whatever she wants to do to let off steam. But after that, she needs her friends around her," Faith said firmly.

Faith left the main building and made her way slowly across the campus. It was a beautiful, starry night, and if it hadn't been for all the trucks and equipment around, the campus would have looked like a fairyland. She picked her way around a giant coil of cable lying on the sidewalk, and thought that Horace Canby would be shocked to see what had happened to his estate in the last few days.

Horace Canby was a wealthy industrialist who had founded Canby Hall in 1897. The property had been intended as a legacy for his daughter, Julia. When she died of fever, he decided to establish a girls' school on the grounds as a memorial to her.

It was hard to believe that the school had grown from thirty girls to two hundred and fifty, Faith thought. In the beginning, there was just the main building for classes, and Baker House was the only dormitory. The science building and library had been added in the 1900s, but some of the campus remained untouched by time. The maple grove and birch grove dated back to Horace Canby's day, and Patrice Allardyce, the headmistress, lived in the Canby family home on the edge of the campus.

That might be a good angle for my story, Faith thought. The old and the new, tradition and innovation. Who would ever think that Hollywood would come to a campus where they did quaint things like make apple butter and maple syrup. *Canby Hall will never be the same,* she mused, walking up the steps to Baker House. And somehow, just somehow, she had to get permission to take pictures. So far, she'd met with stony silence from the production crew. No one wanted to do an interview, and no one wanted to be photographed. That was the official word from Miss Allardyce. However, if the situation changed, they would certainly contact her. *The old "don't-call-us-we'll-call-you" routine,* Faith thought disgustedly. Something had to give!

CHAPTER SIX

I can't believe I got chosen for call-backs," Shelley said on the following Monday. "It dosen't make sense." Everybody had hit the salad bar after looking at the cafeteria special, a murky stew that Dana called Swamp Soup. Shelley speared an olive and looked at it speculatively. "I wonder if I should lose a pound or so by the weekend? Olives are fourteen calories each."

"With or without the pimento?" Faith deadpanned.

"You look great," Dana said firmly. It was true that Shelley had been a little on the plump side when she had first come to Canby Hall, but she now had a slim figure to go with her new wardrobe.

"I just wish the call-backs were right away," Shelley said. "The suspense is going to kill me."

"Hi, everybody." Pamela plunked her tray down across from Casey, and ignored the icy look she got. "What's going to kill you?" she said.

Dana sighed. *Why did Pamela have to pick our table?* she thought, annoyed. *She must think all of us are stupid, or have short memories!* "Shelley got picked for call-backs," she said, finally. "But they're not till next week."

"That's perfect." Pamela smiled. "Because Yvonne is flying in on Saturday, and I know she'd love to coach you."

"Coach me?" Shelley stammered. "I told you, I'll probably die on the spot just before meeting her."

"Honestly, Shelley, what am I going to do with you?" Pamela said, pretending to be annoyed. "You're going to be spending a lot of time around movie stars, so you better get used to it, remember?"

Shelley looked a little embarrassed. "Well, I know we talked about a lot of possibilitiies, but. . . ."

"Don't worry. They'll all come true," Pamela said breezily. She glanced around the table. "How did everybody else do?"

"Dana and I stayed out of the rat race," Faith volunteered. "And Casey's . . ." She stopped and thought. "Atmosphere. Isn't that what you call it?"

"Yeah," Casey said with a grin. "It took me awhile to figure out what that meant. It's a fancy word for an extra."

"What scene are you in?" Pamela said, toying with her lettuce.

"The party scene."

"Well, at least you'll get to wear nice clothes." She smiled innocently, and stared at Casey's faded jeans and T-shirt. It was impossible to know if she was making a crack or not.

"How about you, Pamela? Are you getting a part?" Casey was pretty sure of the answer, but she couldn't resist asking anyway.

"Oh, I'm sure something will turn up for me," Pamela said smoothly.

"I'm sure it will," Casey said under her breath. "Like maybe the lead."

There was an awkward pause and then Dana said reluctantly, "Well, I hate to break this up, gang, but I've got a history paper due tomorrow." She grabbed an apple from the tray. "I've got a fascinating evening planned at the library."

"The library, huh?" Faith raised her eyebrows. "Don't make any detours," she teased. "I heard they're filming a scene down there tonight."

"Don't worry," Dana assured her. "I've got about three hours work ahead of me. By nine o'clock, I've got to be an expert on the Holy Roman Empire."

It was funny, Dana thought, as she picked her way along the icy walk, everyone seemed to be bitten by the acting bug. Everyone but her and Faith. Sure, it was fun to see all the commotion on campus, and do some celebrity-watching, but Alison was right. The movie company *was* a passing thing.

As she approached the library, she spotted a group of actors and technicians gathered on the lawn. Spotlights were mounted in the trees, and the area was so bright it could have been daytime. A couple of catering trucks were set up, and they were serving food on long, wooden tables set up on sawhorses. Faith was right, she thought idly, they must be filming at night. . . .

Suddenly two things happened at once. She heard someone yell "Watch it!" just as she felt herself being hurled through space. She landed ungracefully in a snowdrift, and stood up, feeling foolish.

A young man rushed up to her, and tried to brush the snow off her. "I'm so sorry. It was really stupid of me to leave that cable lying there. I hope you're not hurt." His voice was low and exciting, and he had a terrific British accent, Dana noticed.

"I'll live," Dana said. "I guess I should have watched where I was going." She stared at the young man. He really was unusually handsome, with black hair and flashing, dark eyes.

"It was my fault, believe me." He gave her a devastating smile, and she wondered why he wasn't a movie star himself. If there was such a thing as magnetism, he certainly had it, she caught herself thinking.

"Don't worry about it." She picked up her

books, and smiled at him. "See, no broken bones." She started down the path again when he stopped her.

"I'm Peter Marks," he said and stuck out his hand. "When I nearly get someone killed, I like to at least introduce myself properly."

Dana laughed. He was more than cute. He was funny and a good talker. "I'm Dana Morrison, and I really am okay."

"You're more than okay," he told her, moving a little closer. "I'd say you're absolutely fantastic. I'm a sucker for girls with long, dark hair."

He was a fast worker, Dana thought, a little disconcerted. For once in her life, she couldn't think of anything to say, and he jumped in to fill the gap. "I'll bet you haven't had dinner," he said.

"Just a salad," she said, and felt like biting her tongue off. She was playing right into his hands, and she knew it.

"I could tell," he said, taking her arm. "Girls are always starving themselves. Well, you're in luck, because it's roast beef night." He led her up to the buffet table. "Courtesy of Foxfire Productions. At least they feed us well."

"I . . . I can't have dinner with you," Dana protested.

"Why not?" He gave her an innocent smile.

"I'm not part of the cast or crew. I'm just a student."

"Call it good public relations," he said

firmly and filled a plate for her. "Hold this," he said, and piled his own plate high. "Now let's find someplace where we can sit and talk."

The next hour passed like a dream for Dana. She could hardly believe it. She was sitting having dinner with the cast and crew of a major motion picture. Just like she was one of them! She looked around the long picnic table. They were just people, she realized with a shock. Warm, friendly, open . . . maybe a little tired after the long hours of shooting. But they greeted her with a smile, and no one seemed to think it odd that she was sitting there.

And then there was Peter. She would have liked to talk to him all night, but he got into an animated conversation with a stunt man about car crashes and burning buildings, and she could only listen politely. He smiled at her every now and then, though, as if he was glad she was there. He insisted on getting her coffee and dessert, too.

Finally a young man picked up a megaphone and said wearily, "Okay, everybody. Places, please." There was a groan from the crowd, and he managed a tired smile. "I know, but if we're lucky, we can finish tonight by eleven."

"That's my cue," Peter said, picking up their empty plates.

"I don't know how to thank you for dinner," Dana said. She felt strangely tongue-tied around this exciting young man. For the first time in her life, she felt a little unsure of herself, and she didn't know why. It was something about Peter, she decided. He was so . . . magnetic. That was the only word for it.

He gave her another one of those fantastic smiles. "It was my pleasure, Dana. I'll try not to dump you in any more snowdrifts."

She nodded and didn't say anything. She didn't want to leave him, but couldn't think of any excuse to stay. "Well, uh, I guess I better get to the library. Thanks again for everything." Why did she mention the library? It made her sound like she was twelve years old. At the rate she was going, she'd never see him again. Not unless she managed to get herself knocked out by a sound boom.

Maybe he sensed her hesitation, because he reached out and touched her arm. "We're filming down by the lake tomorrow. Around three. Maybe you'd like to watch." His voice was elaborately casual, but Dana was thrilled. This was all the encouragement she needed.

"I'll be there," she said breathlessly. She practically skipped the rest of the way to the library.

CHAPTER SEVEN

Rock music blasted through Baker House lounge the following Saturday afternoon. It was a cold, blustery day, and the lounge was crammed full of girls watching American Bandstand and nibbling popcorn. Dana, Faith, and Casey were sprawled on an overstuffed sofa waiting for Shelley when suddenly Faith nudged Casey in the ribs. "Look who's coming up the steps," she said, motioning to the leaded glass window. "It's little Miss Hollywood herself, and she's brought her mother!"

"You mean Pamela?" Dana breathed softly. *I'm glad Shelley's not here,* she thought. *She'd freak out being near her idol — the great Yvonne Young.*

"The one and only," Faith said grimly. "I think we're in for a round of bowing and scraping. It's too late to scoot back upstairs."

A moment later, the front door burst open, and Yvonne Young made her entrance. "Oh, how quaint! I just love it!" She stood stock-still, taking in the wood paneling, the oriental rugs, and antique brass lamps. "It's like something out of Dickens."

If she had hoped to make a dramatic first impression, she'd succeeded. All conversation stopped as she posed by the heavy oak door. She was a tall, slim woman with silver blonde hair that tumbled all the way to her shoulders. She was wearing a beige suede pantsuit that was fringed and beaded, and a ton of silver Apache jewelry.

"She's certainly striking-looking," Dana whispered.

"Not to me, she's isn't," Faith insisted. "She looks like she's trying out for the part of Pocahontas."

"Sssh, she'll hear you," Dana said, trying not to giggle. "And look, the two of them are headed this way."

Pamela whispered something, and started to guide her mother right toward them. Her eyes flickered over the astonished faces of the girls in the lounge, and it was obvious that she loved the effect her mother was having on everyone.

"You mean I'm going to get a chance to meet your little friends? Oh, how fun!" Yvonne was saying loudly. She made her way slowly across the room, smiling and nodding like she was a queen greeting her subjects.

"This is my mother," Pamela said, a moment later. She was standing close to Yvonne, and the similarity was startling, Faith thought. They both had the same streaky blonde hair, the same perfect features. And they both were as sleek and self-assured as cats. *Cats with fangs!* Faith reminded herself.

"Hello, darlings," Yvonne cooed at the three of them, as they scrambled to their feet. "Pamela has told me so-o-o much about you."

Dana and Faith exchanged a look. *I'll bet!* Faith's expression said.

"Let me see if I can guess who's who," Yvonne went on. "You must be Dana," she said, "because you have that special New York look." She turned to Pamela who was carrying a fur coat and a giant makeup bag. "You can always tell New York girls," she said gaily. "They have so much style, so much sophistication!" Her eyes swept over Dana's braid belt and handmade jewelry.

"Hello, Mrs. Young," Dana said politely, but Yvonne had already moved on to Faith.

"And you must be Faith," she said, smiling sweetly.

"Right on," Faith muttered. For some reason, she had taken an instant dislike to the woman, and had to force herself to be polite.

"I knew it!" Yvonne said, and clapped her hands together delightedly.

It wouldn't take a Sherlock Holmes to figure it out, Faith thought ironically. *I'm the only black girl in the group.*

Then Yvonne spotted Casey. "And you, my dear, must be Shelley." She gave another of her famous smiles, and Pamela said quickly, "No mother, that's not Shelley. That's Casey Flint."

Yvonne's smile vanished. "Oh, I am sorry!" She gave a withering look to Pamela. "You said Shelley was blonde, so naturally I thought —"

"I'm Shelley," the real Shelley said breathlessly. Everybody turned to look at her. She was dressed in a bright red jogging suit and tennis shoes, and had come up silently behind them. "Gosh, this is fantastic. It's a real honor for you to meet me, Mrs. Young." She clapped her hand over her mouth when she realized what she had said. "I mean, it's an honor for me to meet you."

"Nonsense, my dear. You had it right the first time." Yvonne laughed prettily, showing her perfect teeth, and Shelley looked like she was ready to faint on the spot.

I'm surprised she doesn't curtsy, Faith thought disgustedly. *I should have known she'd simper in front of a real live movie star!*

"Well," Yvonne said briskly, "now that we've all been introduced, why don't I take everybody out to dinner? I couldn't bear to eat the cardboard food on the plane, and I'm absolutely famished."

"Thanks, Mrs. Young, but we already have plans for tonight," Faith said flatly. "We were going to hit Pizza Pete's, weren't we, Shelley?" She looked steadily at Shelley, wondering what she would do.

Shelley hesitated, and Faith felt like smacking her, hard. "I didn't know it was definite. . . ." she hedged. She couldn't take her eyes off Yvonne Young. She was even more beautiful in person than she was on the screen!

There was a pause, and then Yvonne flashed another one of her famous smiles. "Oh, well, I couldn't face pizza, darlings. Tell me, Pamela," she said, "what was the name of that little French restaurant you told me about? Maybe they can do a steak au poivre for us."

"The Auberge," Pamela said. "It's nothing remarkable," she added, sounding just like her mother, "but the steak is pretty good. You are coming with us, aren't you, Shel? I know my mother wants to give you some tips on acting." She smiled at Shelley, and pointedly turned her back on the other three girls.

Shelley nodded, too overcome to speak. She was going to dinner with Yvonne Young! It was like a dream come true. "Let me just get changed," she said, glancing at Faith and Dana's surprised faces. She felt her own face go red with shame but she turned away quickly and dashed upstairs without a word to her friends.

"Can you believe it?" Faith muttered a few minutes later. She and Casey and Dana were strolling across the campus, heading for Pizza Pete's. Without Shelley. "I knew this would happen," she said darkly. "When Shelley gets near a celebrity, she goes nuts!"

"Maybe she can't help it," Dana said. "You know how she is about acting. She always says it's her grand passion in life. Don't forget, she even traded her boyfriend Paul and his tractor for it."

"That's true," Casey said with a grin. "Remember what she was like when we first met her? She wanted to be a farmer's wife. She could hardly wait to get back home to Iowa and watch boll weevils, or whatever they do there."

"And now she wants a fabulous career on the silver screen," Dana said with a sigh. "Well, I just hope things work out for her," she added. "But I'd feel better if she wasn't counting on Pamela."

"If she counts on Pamela for anything, she's got a short memory," Faith said sharply.

Meanwhile, Shelley was having the time of her life at the Auberge. She was so nervous and happy, she could hardly eat, even though Yvonne had ordered charbroiled New York strip steaks for them.

"Well, tell me what you've been doing, darling," Yvonne said, after the waiter had left. "You and your friend have parts in the movie, don't you?" Yvonne sipped a glass of white wine and looked at her daughter expectantly.

"Uh, not yet, mother." Pamela hesitated. "We just had auditions a couple of nights ago."

Yvonne laughed. "Oh, don't be silly. That's just a formality. Of course you all have parts, if you want them."

Shelley stared at her in amazement. She made it all sound so easy! *Maybe everything is easy, if you're a movie star.*

"Shelley was chosen for call-backs," Pamela said. "I'm so happy for her."

"Pamela gave me a lot of help," Shelley said quickly. "I still get really nervous at auditions." She gave a little laugh. "In fact, I don't know how I'll get through another one."

"Of course you will, Shelley." Yvonne reached over and patted her hand. "The trick is not to think of an audition as an ordeal —"

"But it is!" Shelley blurted out. "It's like going to the dentist."

Yvonne shook her head and smiled. "No, that's where you're wrong, Shelley. It's an opportunity. An audition is a chance to show the producer or casting director how talented you are."

"That's really all there is to it?" Shelley said, surprised.

Yvonne shrugged and gave one of her musical laughs. "It worked for me, didn't it?"

The waiter served a giant tossed salad and did a doubletake when he noticed Yvonne. "Are you . . . are you. . . . ?"

Pamela sighed as if this was a familiar scene. "She's Yvonne Young," she said.

"I knew it!" the waiter said excitedly. "Can I have your autograph? Wait till I tell them back in the kitchen!" He whipped out an order pad for Yvonne to sign. "I've seen every one of your movies — twice!"

"That's nice," Yvonne said. She signed her name with a flourish and the waiter was so thrilled he almost knocked over the water glasses. When he left, she turned to Shelley. "Always give autographs," she said. "A lot of actresses don't bother, but remember, it's the fans who keep you working."

"I'll remember," Shelley said. She was really impressed. Not only was Pamela's mother a terrific actress, she was also a very nice person. And she talked to her like she was a grown-up, an equal. She looked at Pamela and sighed. She wondered if she realized how lucky she was to have a mother like Yvonne Young.

Pamela must have felt her eyes on her, because she turned and gave her a puzzled smile. Shelley stared at her. She looked very pretty in the soft candlelight of the Auberge with her fair skin and spun-gold hair. It was hard to believe that she'd played such nasty tricks on all of them, just a short time ago, Shelley thought. She'd lied and cheated, and done everything she could to break up their friendship.

But Pamela seemed different now, didn't

she? After all, she had practically guaranteed her a part in the movie. Yvonne Young asked her a question about Canby Hall then, and Shelley forced her mind back to the present. It was silly to dwell on old grudges. She was having dinner with a movie star, and it was the best evening of her whole life!

It wasn't until much later that night, that Shelley realized her roommates didn't share her enthusiasm for Pamela's mother. She was coming out of the fourth floor shower, when she heard Dana say, "Well, was Yvonne better or worse than you expected?"

"She was exactly what I expected," Faith answered. "A little Hollywood, a little phony. Very impressed with herself. She's like an older version of Pamela. Why? What did you think of her?"

"I guess she does seem a little . . . theatrical . . . but that's just part of her job, isn't it?" She paused. "I mean, actors and actresses really do seem different than the rest of us, don't they?"

Faith shrugged. "Maybe," she said non-committally. "But as far as I'm concerned, she and Pamela are two peas in a pod."

"Well, I think she's fabulous," Shelley said angrily, bursting in from the hall with a towel wrapped around her. "You don't know her at all. I spent the whole evening with her, and she's wonderful. Really down to earth. And she thinks that I may have real talent!" She was really getting fed up with her friends. It was true that Pamela had almost broken up their friendship once before, but it wasn't fair to blame Yvonne for it.

"Just don't go overboard," Dana said cautiously. "She hasn't even see you act. . . ."

"Are you saying I don't have talent?" Shelley said indignantly. Her blue eyes were blazing.

"No, of course not. I just mean. . . ."

"You just mean you haven't seen any sign of it yet. Well, just you wait, Dana Morrison, because you will!"

She stormed back into the bathroom for the hair dryer, and Dana looked helplessly at Faith. "What did I say?"

"Don't worry about it," Faith told her. She sighed and closed her history book. "I think we're in for a tough few weeks."

CHAPTER EIGHT

"That has got to be the world's quickest break," Peter said, and drained his coffee cup. It was late Sunday afternoon and Dana had spent practically the whole day waiting to talk to him. They were filming a scene in the maple grove, and a light snow had started to fall.

"You have to go back to work already?" Dana wailed. "We just started talking." She stomped her feet to get warm, and wished she had remembered to wear mittens.

"I know," he said ruefully. "Things were just getting interesting. But you know what they say. Duty calls." He sighed and picked up a length of cable. "I've got to mike someone for the next scene."

"Mike them?"

Peter smiled. "Put one of these gizmos on them." He showed her a tiny microphone. "You thread it through their clothes. If you do it right, no one even notices. Sometimes it's better to do it this way instead of using the big boom mike."

"I see," Dana said through chattering teeth. She was trying to sound impressed, but she was secretly disgusted. At the rate she was going, she'd never get a chance to know Peter Marks. She'd been hanging around for hours, hoping to get a few minutes to talk to him. But she quickly discovered that the "breaks" in the movie business were few and far between. "How many more scenes are you going to shoot today?" she asked. "You're not going to shoot in the dark, are you?"

"I don't know," he said. "I've got to check the board." He paused and looked down at her. "I'd really like to spend some time with you, though, Dana."

She stared up into his fantastic dark eyes, and almost forgot that her hands were getting numb. "I'd like that, too," she said unsteadily. "But I don't know how we'll work it out. You never seem to have any time off."

He rubbed his chin thoughtfully. "You could join me, you know."

"What do you mean?" Out of the corner of her eye, Dana could see a technician walking purposefully toward them. In another minute, Peter would be back at work.

"Well, you could be part of the movie. It would be a lot easier to see you then. We'd be working on the same scenes together, and it would be easy to get you invitations to the cast parties."

"I could be in the movie?"

"Sure." He laughed and tapped her under the chin. "Why not? You're a beautiful girl. I thought all American girls want to grow up to be movie stars. Or do they want to be Miss America?"

"Hey Peter," a bearded cameraman said brusquely, "quit jabbering and get Laura miked. They're ready to start." He stared with open curiosity at Dana.

"I've got to go," Peter said with a grin. "But think about what I said, okay? They're doing the final casting tonight."

Dana nodded. "I know. My roommate was chosen for call-backs."

"Well, just remember. I'd like to spend some time with you. A lot of time." He grinned at her and strode off.

Dana stood for a moment, watching him. He was sensational, she thought. One in a thousand. She smiled to herself, thinking of the boys she had met during the past year. First there was Bret Harper, Oakley Prep's resident playboy. He'd been a real heart-breaker. She could still remember their big good-bye scene. It had felt exactly like some-one twisting a giant knife in her chest, but she had recovered. And lived to smile about it.

Then there was Randy, a nice guy who turned out to be not a boyfriend, but a great pal. And there were a few casual dates in between. But there was no one — absolutely no one, she decided — who could hold a candle to Peter Marks.

But could she really get a part in the movie? She'd have to audition, and everyone would wonder why she changed her mind, and. . . . Suddenly she spotted Peter at the far end of the set. He adjusted a light, and was making his way back to the camera. His movements were quick and graceful, his body lean and hard in jeans and a navy sweater. He must have felt Dana's eyes on him, because he looked at her and gave a heartstopping grin.

That does it, she decided. *I'm getting a part in the movie. Somehow, I've got to get in on call-backs.* . . . She hurried back to the dorm, with a plan half-forming in her head.

By seven-thirty that night, Shelley was a nervous wreck. "You'd think she was appearing on Broadway," Faith said half-jokingly to Casey. "She's done everything to her face except trade it in for a new one."

"Don't give her any ideas," Dana pleaded. "She's washed and set her hair so many times today, she's probably shortened its life." Dana hadn't said a word to her roommates about her decision to be in the movie. She had decided that the fewer people who knew the better.

The three girls were sprawled on the floor mattresses in 407 waiting for Shelley to make her big entrance from the bathroom. Finally the door opened, and a pale, shaky Shelley emerged.

"Isn't Pamela here yet?" she asked plaintively. "She said she'd come by to pick me up."

Dana and Faith exchanged a look. Neither one of them trusted Pamela an inch, but it was impossible to criticize her in front of Shelley.

"Shelley, we'll walk over to the audition with you. Nothing like a little moral support, you know," Faith said, trying to get a smile out of her. "Just think. You'll be the only girl there with her own fan club." She grinned encouragingly at Shelley, but got a blank look in reply.

"I'd feel better if Pamela was here," Shelley insisted.

"I wouldn't," Casey said cheerfully. Casey and Pamela tried to steer clear of one another whenever possible.

"Well, it's time," Dana said, swinging her long legs off the bed. "Let's go, gang."

"Why do I feel like I'm going to my execution?" Shelley said, as they hurried toward the main building.

"Stop worrying," Faith told her. "You're going to be sensational." Faith gave Shelley's arm a little squeeze. "And when it's over, we'll break out the brownies and celebrate."

"I just hope there's something to celebrate," Shelley said quietly. "I've never felt so nervous in my life. Did you hear what Carol said?

They're having us read with real actors tonight. Real stars! I'll die. I just know I will."

"Nonsense," Dana said firmly. "You'll be great. Now go!" They opened the heavy door to the main building, and practically pushed Shelley inside. A dozen or so girls were standing in the hall, talking.

"They must have weeded out a lot of people," Casey whispered, glancing around. "There's hardly anybody here."

"Let's just hope they don't weed out Shelley," Faith said grimly. "Getting this part means everything to her."

"Where do I go for call-backs?" Shelley asked a woman wearing a Foxfire T-shirt.

"First, you have to sign in down at Room 102," the woman told her. "Then in a few minutes, they'll call you into Room 101 to read for them." She stared at Faith and Casey. "Your friends can wait for you right here."

"Okay, fine," Shelley gulped. She looked as white as a sheet and Dana felt a pang of sympathy for her. It was funny that Pamela hadn't shown up, Dana thought suddenly. But then Pamela had always been unpredictable. And selfish.

"So, I guess this is it. Wish me luck. No, I mean, wish that I break a leg." Shelley tried to grin, but her lower lip was trembling.

"Hey, you'll be great," her friends chorused. "Go on, don't keep Hollywood waiting," Casey said. Shelley finally headed down to

Room 102 alone, and Casey and Faith sat crosslegged on the floor.

It was at that moment that Dana decided to put her plan into action. If she was ever going to get a part in the movie, now was the time to do it. She pretended to be fascinated by some class pictures hanging at the far end of the hall.

"Hey, Dana," Faith said, when she saw Dana wandering away. "Where are you going? We're supposed to meet Shelley when she gets back."

Dana turned and gave a mysterious smile. "Oh, I just want to take a look around." She turned the corner, and headed quickly in the direction of Room 102. She knew she had to move fast, and she didn't want to have to explain things to Casey and Faith.

Shelley had just signed in, when she heard a familiar voice behind her.

"Michelle, I'm so glad I caught you. Gosh, I'm ever so sorry I was late. My mother got a call from the Coast, and would you believe Matt Dillon wanted to wish me luck? Isn't that cute?" She threw her head back and laughed in a very theatrical way.

Shelley was too nervous to be impressed. "I thought you were going to give me some last-minute advice," she said reproachfully.

"Well, sweetie, I am," Pamela said very seriously. She pulled Shelley away from a group of girls who were listening to every word. "Listen," she said, lowering her voice to almost a whisper. "I got the scoop on Albritton."

"The director?" Shelley said.

"Yes, of course, the director," Pamela said, impatiently. "Yvonne has worked with him before, and the trick is to underplay everything."

"Underplay everything," Shelley repeated solemnly.

"Absolutely. You know the old saying that 'less is more'? Well, he practically invented it. He likes everything scaled down, really low-key." Pamela grinned. "In fact, if you practically whisper your lines with no expression, you're guaranteed a part. He simply can't stand actors who overdo it." She paused and looked at Shelley. "Have you got that?"

"I hope so." A woman with a clipboard was coming toward her. Shelley knew she was next, and she felt like falling through the floor.

"Remember, underplay it," Pamela hissed.

A moment later, Shelley found herself in Room 101. Everything looked familiar — the long table, the three judges, the stacks of scripts. But this time there was something different. Troy Adams. A real, live movie star!

There was a rumor going around that he would be on campus, but Shelley hadn't believed it. It just seemed too incredible that he would actually show up at Canby Hall.

But here he was. She took one look at the

fabulous Troy Adams and felt more terrified than ever. If ever there was such a thing as "star quality," she thought, Troy had it. In fact, he had everything, she admitted. He was tall, and good-looking, and he had a fantastic smile. All his movies had been big box-office hits.

And he was standing just inches away from her.

"Page thirty-two. Susan. Take it from the top," someone said in a weary voice. Shelley felt like she was rooted to the floor, but it didn't matter, because Troy shoved a script in her hand.

"Is it true what they say about sorority girls?" he said in a low, sexy voice.

For a crazy moment, she thought he was making conversation. Then she realized her mistake, and she scanned the script, desperately trying to find her place.

"I don't know what you're talking about," she said, and gave a nervous laugh. The script said she was supposed to be "flirtatious," but that was out of the question. It took all her concentration just to say the lines! Luckily, she remembered what Pamela had told her. Downplay everything. She relaxed a little, then. If the director wanted understatement, he'd get understatement.

"I think you do," he went on. His eyes locked with hers, and she could barely focus on the script.

"Maybe I should ask you about fraternity

boys," she said quietly. "I've heard about all those wild parties." She kept her voice very flat, just like Pamela said. She didn't even smile. "I went to a fraternity weekend last spring with my roommate, and we —"

"Okay, thank you," someone cut in. Shelley looked up blankly, not sure who had spoken. "That's it," a voice repeated. The people at the table were making notes. Either she had played the part exactly right, and it was hers, or. . . . She put the script back on the table and turned to leave. Suddenly the door opened and Dana came in. Dana! What was she doing here? Shelley stared at her in amazement. A moment later, the mystery was cleared up.

"Miss Morrison?" Carol Gate peered at Dana through aviator glasses. "Would you read the part of Susan for us?"

Shelley's mind was racing. Susan! That was the part she had just read. And Dana hadn't been chosen for call-backs. She hadn't even auditioned. What was going on?

"Uh, that's all, Miss Hyde," Carol said to her. She realized she was supposed to leave, but she felt like she had cement blocks on her feet. "You can go now."

Shelley nodded and made her way to the door as slowly as she could. But not before she had a chance to hear Dana read the same lines she had just read. They were competing for the same part!

"Why, I don't know what you're talking

about," she heard Dana say to Troy. "You fraternity boys are all alike!" Her voice was smooth, like honey, and she had just the right teasing edge to it. She didn't try to underplay it, either. She moved so close to Troy she was practically standing on top of him and grinned up at him. "I've heard about your wild parties," she went on. Her eyes never left his face, and Troy was smiling back at her.

Where had Dana learned to act? Shelley hated to admit it, but Dana was good. Then she remembered what Pamela had said about Tony Albritton. He liked everything underplayed, everything low-key. And Dana's performance was anything but low-key. He'd hate it. She breathed a sigh of relief. She was sure the part was still hers.

CHAPTER NINE

By the time Shelley got back to the dorm, she was more puzzled than ever by Dana's behavior. Why in the world had she decided to audition? And why hadn't she told anyone? The more she thought about it, the more angry she got.

"It just seems so sneaky and underhanded," she complained to Faith. The two of them were attacking a box of butterscotch brownies that Faith's mother had sent from home. Casey had walked back to Baker House with them, grabbed a brownie, and then zipped up to her own room to study.

"Well, it may look that way, but you know that Dana's not like that," Faith said slowly. "In fact, she's one of the most upfront people I know."

"Usually," Shelley said darkly. "And I wonder why she's taking so long?" she said, glancing at her watch. "It's funny, I was only in there for a minute."

Faith gave her a worried look. "Is that a good sign? I mean, I don't know anything about auditions, but I thought —"

"Oh, it's a good sign," Shelley said breezily. "You see, Pamela told me exactly what they were looking for. I got the straight scoop on how to read for the part."

Faith nodded and didn't answer. As far as she could see, *Midnight Whispers* was causing nothing but problems for the girls in 407. There were disappointments all around. Shelley was going to feel terrible if she didn't get a part, and as for herself — she still hadn't gotten permission to take a single picture for the *Clarion!* The movie business was a big headache, she decided, reaching for another brownie.

Suddenly, the door burst open, and a flushed-looking Dana came in.

"Well, here she is at last," Shelley said coolly. "And what was that all about?"

Dana peeled off her coat. "You mean the audition?" she said innocently.

"Yes, I mean the audition!" Shelley folded her arms in front of her. Her blue eyes were icy. "Your little surprise move. How come you never said a word to us? I didn't know that you had a secret desire to be a movie star."

"I didn't, either," Dana admitted. She opened a can of diet soda, and helped herself to a brownie. "In fact, I don't. It's kind of a long story." She flopped on the mattress, suddenly bone-tired. She felt too tired for a long, drawn-out explanation, but she knew that Shelley wouldn't take no for an answer.

"That's all right," Shelley said sarcastically. "We have all night."

"Okay," Dana said wearily. "I'll try to explain." She kicked off her shoes and tucked a pillow behind her head. "I met someone." She smiled, thinking of Peter and the way he looked at her with those flashing, dark eyes. "Someone connected with the movie."

Shelley and Faith stared at her. "And who is this mysterious someone? Does he have a name?" Shelley said bitingly.

Dana sighed. She couldn't figure out why Shelley was acting so upset, as if she had done something terrible. "His name is Peter Marks and he's a technician."

"You're kidding! You mean you went after a part in the movie because of some guy you met?" Shelley was staring at her in disbelief.

"If you met him, you'd know why," Dana said drily. "And he's not some guy. He's fantastic."

"Well, it seems like a crazy reason to be an actress," Shelley said flatly. She was starting to feel a little better about the whole thing. Poor Dana wanted a part in *Midnight Whispers* so she could see her new boyfriend, and she didn't stand a chance! There was no sense in dashing her hopes, though. She'd find out soon enough. "You sounded pretty good at the audition," she said generously.

"Thanks," Dana said quietly. "I got the part."

For a moment no one spoke. Faith stared from Dana to Shelley like she was watching a tennis match. *Uh-oh,* she thought. *Fireworks.*

"You what!" Shelley demanded.

"I said I got the part," Dana repeated calmly. "They had me read for the part of Susan three times, and they finally said I had it. We start filming tomorrow."

"I can't believe it." Shelley sank onto her mattress, afraid she was going to break into tears.

Dana stared at her. "Which part did you read for?"

"Susan," Shelley said in a small voice.

"Shelley, I had no idea," Dana said, aghast. "You and I are completely different. We don't look anything alike, or sound alike." She looked helplessly at Faith. "I never dreamed we'd be trying out for the same part."

"How did you work it, anyway?" Faith said, curious. "You never even auditioned, and yet you got into call-backs tonight."

"Oh, that," Dana said, a little embarrassed. "I just told them that I got a notice in my mailbox to come to call-backs." She shrugged. "They didn't even question it."

"So being sneaky pays off," Shelley said suddenly, looking up. Her eyes looked suspiciously bright, as if she was going to start crying any minute.

"C'mon, Shel," Faith said. "I know you're disappointed, but it's kind of silly to attack Dana. You probably would have done the same thing."

"Maybe, maybe not." She reached for her hairbrush and started slowly brushing her curly blonde hair. "It would depend on how much I cared about my friends." She glared at Dana.

"This is crazy," Dana said. She was starting to get mad. "Shelley, I told you I had no idea we'd be competing for the same part. I figured there were dozens of parts."

"There aren't dozens of parts," Shelley said. "If you'd paid any attention to the notices, you would have realized that."

"But I wasn't even interested in any of this until I met Peter," Dana said. "Honestly! How can I be blamed for wanting to see him?"

"You can't be," Faith said quietly. She looked at Shelley. "And I think if Shelley thinks it over, she'll realize that." When Shelley didn't answer, Faith sighed and said, "Look, it's ten o'clock. I think we should all get a good night's sleep, okay?" She managed a giant yawn even though she wasn't tired. "You know what they say about things looking better in the morning." She smiled hopefully at her roommates, but no one was paying any attention to her.

Suddenly Shelley bounded off the bed, grabbed a towel, and headed for the fourth floor shower. After she slammed the door,

Dana and Faith exchanged a look. "Thanks for trying," Dana said quietly. "I think she's going to stay mad for a long time, though."

Meanwhile, Shelley stood under the jet of hot water, and the steam rose around her like a cloud. She squinted her eyes shut, and tried not to think, feeling pins and needles in her arms and legs. How could she have let such a great part slip away from her? It was all some awful mistake. Dana wasn't the actress, she was. She was the one who had taken the summer intensive, she was the one with the real talent. She stopped, and felt tears well up in her eyes. No, it wasn't a mistake. It was silly to make excuses, to try to make sense out of what had happened. She had blown it. Period.

When her skin turned lobster-red from the scalding water, she slowly got out and wrapped a towel around her. She stared at herself in the mirror. She looked the same as always. You'd never know she had just had the biggest disappointment of her whole life, she thought ruefully. And she had done it all by herself.

Except . . . what about Pamela? She frowned, remembering what Pamela had told her earlier that night. "Underplay everything," she had said. "You're practically guaranteed a part." She had been very definite about it.

But Dana overplayed it and got the part! Was Pamela wrong about what the director really wanted? Did she give her bad advice on purpose? Somehow, she'd have to get at the truth. . . .

Back in 407, Dana hurriedly put on her pajamas and slipped into bed. She switched off her night light and pretended to be asleep. The last thing she wanted was another confrontation with Shelley. She could hardly believe it! Shelley actually blamed her for taking the part away from her.

Dana sighed and buried her head in the soft pillow. She had never thought that things would get this complicated. The last thing in the world she wanted was to make trouble for her roommate. After all, she wasn't starstruck like Shelley, and she really didn't care if she was in the movie or not. Except for Peter. She thought of his broad shoulders and sexy voice. He made it all worthwhile. She could hardly wait to tell him they'd be spending a lot of time together. It was hard to believe she'd see him the next day. . . .

Faith tried to read, and finally gave up. *I'm glad Shelley's taking a long time in the shower,* she thought. *I just don't feel like another hassle tonight. And I wonder why I'm always the one stuck in the middle!*

Faith's bed was near the window, and she stared out at the moon rising high in the sky. *That would make a great picture,* she thought. *The silvery moon like a silhouette against the inky sky. I should be taking dozens of pictures of the people in the movie com-*

pany. I could photograph the sets, and the extras, and all the technical people — the cameramen and lighting engineers. If only the movie company wasn't so secretive about everything! she thought resentfully. *Every time I ask permission I get turned down. Maybe the best thing to do is just go ahead. Not ask anybody's permssion for anything. . . .* She decided to put her plan into action the very next day.

There was an uneasy truce the next morning in Room 407. The alarm went off at six-thirty, as always, but instead of the usual groans, conversation was at a minimum. Shelley didn't speak to Dana at all, and Dana seemed unusually quiet. Faith decided that she was probably a little embarrassed by the situation. Faith shrugged into a heavy parka and left the room with a quiet "Bye, everybody."

The wind was biting as she walked down the steps of Baker House and headed toward the library, but she was too excited to care. She had made her decision. She was going to put together a portfolio of pictures whether Foxfire Productions liked it or not!

She glanced at her watch. It was a little after seven, but Canby Hall was alive with activity. Forfire production people were milling around the campus, and a silver catering truck was set up in the main quadrangle.

Some extras were crowded around the truck, sipping coffee and stomping their feet to keep warm. Faith thought of photographing them, and then changed her mind. Her first stop would be the makeup tent, she decided. She patted her camera and felt in her pocket for the extra rolls of film.

Just act confident, she reminded herself. *Act like you belong here, and no one will question anything.* When she got to the large brown tent in front of the library, she pushed aside the flap and walked in.

"Hi," she said brightly to a tired-looking man sipping coffee. He was standing all alone in front of a long table that was littered with dozens of jars and tubes and brushes.

"Oh, good, did you bring the doughnuts?" he said hopefully.

Faith looked at him in surprise. "I'm afraid not."

"You're not from catering?" He sighed and took another swig of coffee.

"No, I'm a student. A student here at Canby Hall," she added.

"I should have known," he said, smiling suddenly. "You look like too nice a person to be responsible for this coffee. I think it was brewed by Lucrezia Borgia." He stared thoughtfully into the paper cup.

"Would you mind if I take your picture?" Faith asked, unzipping her camera bag. "Photography is sort of a hobby of mine." She grinned at him. It was probably better not to mention the *Clarion*, she decided. Just act like she was an amateur shutterbug.

"Snap away," he said grandly. He put down the coffee cup, and struck a pose in front of a long mirror. "Alex Hayden, makeup man to the stars," he added with a grin.

Not bad, Faith thought, as the shutter clicked over and over. There was a nice reflection in the mirror, and the early morning light made an interesting pattern as it filtered in the tent. "Would you mind if I sort of hung around, and took some more pictures? When people come in to be made up, I mean?"

"Be my guest. You're the next best thing to doughnuts." He pulled over a stool for her to sit on. "The hordes will be arriving any minute."

No sooner had he spoken, then the flap opened and a thin blonde stuck her head in. "Alex! Can you do some eyes? I've got about six out here. They've done their own base, but they need some eyes."

"Certainly, my dear. Send them in." He winked at Faith. "You'll get some good shots of what people look like without their 'eyes' on. You can do before-and-after shots."

Faith's hand automatically went to her camera, and she changed to a high F-stop number. The blonde had pinned back the flap and the tent was suddenly flooded with light.

"Victim number one," Alex said with a smile, as a young girl with a round face and freckles settled into the chair. He picked up a black eyeliner and started to work. "Cleopatra, eat your heart out," he said.

Faith aimed her camera and took shot after shot. She couldn't believe her luck! Candid shots. Actors without makeup. Early morning calls. Drafty tents. Frowns and yawns. Pale faces and eye-circles. All the unglamorous aspects of the movie business. This was exactly what she was after.

CHAPTER TEN

As soon as Faith left 407, Shelley picked up a bottle of honeysuckle shampoo and stomped off to the shower. Dana was secretly relieved, and threw open the closet doors. With any luck, she could be dressed and out of the room by the time Shelley got back. It was bad enough to think that she'd be facing the cameras that afternoon, but Shelley's martyr act was more than she could take!

She had absolutely no idea what to wear. She tried on her best outfit, a cream-colored wool sweater dress, hated it, and tossed it on the bed. Then she tried some plum velvet seven-eighths pants her mother had sent her from New York. Too far-out, she decided. They might look great on Fifth Avenue, but they looked weird at Canby Hall. Designer jeans with an oversized sweatshirt and hip belt? Too boring. She sighed and stared at the rows of hangers. In a few minutes, Shelley would be back and the deep-freeze treatment would start all over again.

"I shouldn't even be worrying about my clothes," Dana muttered under her breath. She knew that the wardrobe department would give her whatever she needed for her scene. Her main worry should be remembering her lines, and not giving in to a giant case of stage fright. She had done well at the audition, but maybe that was just a lucky break. After all, who knew what would happen once the cameras started rolling?

She finally decided to dress the way she normally did, and bundled up in a bright raspberry sweater, black wool pants, and cowboy boots. A touch of eyeliner and mascara, followed by lip gloss, and she was done. There was no sense in doing anything else, she reasoned, since she'd be reporting to Makeup, anyway.

She quickly reviewed what she had to do that day. Spanish class, a history quiz, and study hall. Then lunch, math, and report to the set for filming. And most important of all, she'd see Peter! They'd actually be working together on a movie. It sounded crazy and impossible. And terrifically exciting. She ran a brush through her long, brown hair, took a quick look in the mirror, and dashed out the door. There was no time for breakfast — she'd be lucky if she made it to Spanish class before the bell rang.

Half an hour later, she stared at Mr. Ramirez and wondered if there really was such a thing as "time standing still." She was sure the old-fashioned wooden clock that hung over the blackboard must be stuck, because every time she looked, it said the same thing.

She sighed and forced herself to return to her Spanish book. They were translating a particularly dull chapter on "Eating Out" and Mr. Ramirez was pretending to be a waiter taking orders for breakfast. Fascinating. What did it matter if she knew how to order in Spanish? Dana thought irritably. They probably didn't even have fried eggs in Spain! She stole another look at the clock. Foxfire had told her to report to the production office at two-thirty sharp. Exactly six hours and seventeen minutes to go. It was going to be a very long morning.

At that precise moment, Shelley was staring listlessly at the cafeteria special. It must be eggs, she decided, because they were almost the right color. Watery yellow. But they weren't scrambled, poached, or fried. . . . They were smothered in a pasty, white sauce. She didn't even know why she'd bothered going to breakfast this morning, except she didn't have an eight o'clock class, and it was too depressing to stay in the room.

"I can't believe it! They've actually attempted eggs Benedict. Will these people *never* learn?" Pamela gave a low, rippling laugh, and pushed her tray up against Shelley's. "I think I'll stick to black coffee. They haven't figured out a way to ruin that yet. But I'm sure they're working on it," she added sweetly to the woman behind the counter. Shelley glanced at her. Pamela looked as glamorous as ever. She was wearing one of her "Rodeo Drive" outfits — skinny black leather pants, and a red T-shirt emblazoned with Japanese letters.

"Hello, Pamela," Shelley said slowly. She didn't know if she should be friendly, or if she should dump her bowl of cornflakes on Pamela's pretty head. She still couldn't get over the fact that Pamela had given her such bad advice — rotten advice, in fact — and that she had lost out on a part in the movie. "I really need to talk to you," she added.

"Well, sure, honey," Pamela said, flashing a thousand-kilowatt smile at her. "I want to hear all about what happened last night." She led Shelley to a table by the window. "Okay, shoot," she said, cradling her cup of steaming coffee. "What part did you get?"

"I didn't get any part!" Shelley blurted out. *So much for being cool and laid-back,* she thought. It meant too much to her to pretend that everything was okay. "I did exactly what you told me," she said accusingly. "I underplayed it. In fact, I underplayed it to death. No smile, no expression, nothing. And guess what? No part."

"Hmm," Pamela said vaguely. She sipped

her coffee, as if her mind were miles away, and didn't say anything.

She doesn't even seem the least bit upset, Shelley thought resentfully. *Just a little puzzled.* "I said, I followed your advice about the audition, Pamela," she repeated. "It didn't work."

Pamela put down her coffee cup, and looked as if she were seeing her for the first time. "Well, I may have misled you a little," she said finally. "Not intentionally, of course," she added when she saw Shelley's expression. "You see, Tony is known for his understatement. . . ."

"Yes, I know," Shelley said impatiently. "And?"

Pamela licked her lips. "Well, it just so happens that in this particular movie, he's . . . uh, looking for a different effect. I mean, he's such a fantastic director, and he's always experimenting with new styles, new techniques. And so you may have underplayed it just a touch too much. I don't think any real harm is done, though," she added breezily. "Maybe you can audition again for him."

"That's crazy," Shelley protested. "The part's gone!"

"Gone?" Pamela said calmly. She peered coolly at Shelley over the rim of her coffee cup.

"Yes, gone. Dana's got it. She's playing the part of Susan. The part I tried out for!"

Pamela shook her head in seeming sympathy. "Oh, gosh, that *is* tough. I'm really sorry. I didn't even know Dana was an actress."

"She's not," Shelley said. "She's got a crush on one of the technicians, Peter somebody, and she figures this is a good way for her to see him." She stared morosely into her corn-flakes.

"Oh, I see." Pamela shrugged and stood up. "Well, I don't know about you, but I've got a nine o'clock. Are you coming?"

"I . . . uh . . . don't feel very well," Shelley said dully. "I may cut this morning." It was practically true, she thought. She'd had a stomachache ever since the audition last night.

"Well, I hope you're not coming down with anything," Pamela said. "After all, you still want a part in the movie, don't you?"

"What? Of course I do!" Shelley brightened. "Do you think there's still a chance?"

Pamela smiled. "Maybe with a word to the right person. I'm sure Yvonne will think of something. Listen," she added, "why don't you meet me at three in front of the production office, and I'll let you know how I made out."

"Okay," Shelley said quickly. She had a math test at three, but that didn't matter. The main thing was to get a part in *Midnight Whispers*. "Do you think I can get another audition?"

"Who knows? Let's see what Yvonne comes

up with. She usually has some pretty good ideas."

After Pamela left, Shelley sat in the cafeteria, lost in thought. She really needed to go to history class, but she just couldn't face it. Not today, of all days. She'd have to make up an excuse, of course, but that shouldn't be too hard. She'd just have to concentrate on getting a part in the movie, and everything else would fall into place.

At two-thirty sharp, Dana stood outside the production office in the main building and took three deep breaths. She remembered reading someplace that that was a trick that actors used to calm down. She took a few more breaths. Still no luck. After fifteen deep breaths, she started to feel dizzy, and she decided she'd better sign in, nervous or not. Her heart was hammering and her knees felt like jelly. *This is what you wanted,* she told herself over and over. *It's a chance to see Peter.*

She was just about to push the door open when Faith pounced on her. "Smile. You're on Candid Camera!" Faith whispered and started clicking away.

"What are you doing?" Dana said, blinking against the popping flashbulb. "I thought you weren't allowed to take any pictures."

"Shhh. I'm not." Faith leaned close to her. "But I decided this was a now-or-never opportunity. I got some terrific shots in the Makeup tent this morning, and a few in Wardrobe, and with a little luck, I'll get some on the set." She stopped talking long enough to peer at Dana. "Hey, what's wrong? You look terrible."

"Thanks," Dana said wryly. "I've been taking deep breaths trying to relax, but they almost did me in."

"I think you've been hyperventilating," Faith giggled. "You look sort of pale and pasty."

"Good. She can play the ghost," Carol Gate said with a grin. She had come up silently behind them in the hallway. "Who's here to sign in?"

"She is," Faith said. "I've got to scoot. I'll catch you later, Dana. I've got to hit the books." She smiled innocently at Carol, and shoved her camera out of sight in the folds of her big winter coat.

"Dana . . . Dana . . . Morrison. Here you are," Carol said, looking at her clipboard. "C'mon inside and let's check the board." She ushered Dana into the production office. There were three young women sitting behind desks answering phones, and a couple of technicians drinking coffee. With a start, Dana realized that one of them was Peter.

"Well, hello," he said, and eased himself out of a canvas chair. "Are you working with us today?"

"I sure am," she said. She could feel an enormous grin spreading over her face, and hoped that Carol Gate wouldn't notice. He was so terrific! It was going to be fantastic to get to work with him, to see him every day. "I got the part of Susan," she told him. She was trying to keep her voice even, and not let all the excitement she felt pour out.

"That's great. Congratulations." He moved very close to her, and gave her arm a little squeeze. His eyes were piercingly black, and there was something about the pale blue sweater that set them off perfectly. She had almost forgotten how handsome he was. "Is she in the birch grove scene, Carol?"

"She sure is." Carol was peering at a giant blackboard. "You'll need to check the callboard every day, Dana," she told her. "Make sure you know what scenes you're supposed to be in, and where we'll be filming. If there's any change, I'll put a note in your mailbox. Okay?"

Dana nodded, and Peter said cheerfully, "I'll make sure she gets to the right place at the right time, Carol. Consider me your personal escort, Dana."

Carol glanced at her watch. "And always check the times carefully, too. Give yourself at least an hour to get to Wardrobe and Makeup, because sometimes things really get jammed over there." Her eyes flicked over Dana's Mexican poncho. "What do you have on under that? Maybe you won't need Wardrobe today."

"A sweater and pants," Dana said, slipping the poncho over her head.

"That's fine. You look great," Carol said. "Okay, head for Makeup and then the birch grove. And here's your script."

"My script?" Dana stammered.

"It's only a couple of lines today," Carol said with a laugh. "You can learn them on the way over. Unless Peter talks your ear off," she said, pretending to glare at him.

"I won't say a word," Peter said, taking her arm. "In fact, I'll help you rehearse." He winked at Carol. "It's not a love scene, by any chance, is it?"

"Sorry, Peter," she sighed. "No such luck."

"Ah well, as you Americans say, you can't win them all."

"I hope I do all right," she told him a few minutes later, as they hurried to the Makeup tent. "I'm not really an actress."

"Well, you got the part, didn't you? You must have impressed somebody," he said reasonably. He stopped in the middle of the walk and stared at her. "Unless you're the daughter of someone terribly rich and famous?" he said teasingly. "Is that how you got the part?"

"Afraid not," she laughed. "I was just lucky. And very determined."

"Two qualities I admire," Peter said. They had gotten to the Makeup tent much sooner than Dana would have liked. "Well, this is where I leave you. At least for half an hour or so."

"But you will be working on this scene,

won't you?" Dana said urgently. She suddenly had butterflies at the idea of being on the set alone.

"Of course I will," he said, and touched her gently on the chin. The sun had disappeared and he was wearing a heavy parka to ward off the cold. "Are you getting cold feet?"

"Yes," she admitted and had to laugh. "Both kinds."

"You've got nothing to worry about," he told her. "Now let Alex do his magic, and I'll see you down at the birch grove." He shivered and blew on his hands. "I had forgotten what New England winters are like. Let's just hope we break early for dinner."

Dinner! Dana had completely forgotten that she'd get to eat with the cast again. How fabulous. Shelley and Faith would be eating back at the dining hall. She felt a little pang of remorse when she remembered Shelley had really wanted this part. *Well*, she thought, *it was fair. We both auditioned. And everything worked out so perfectly. I'll have hours to spend with Peter, first on the set, and then at dinner, and maybe we'd even have time to take a moonlight walk around the lake. . . .*

It was going to be a perfect afternoon and evening. She just knew it. She smiled and walked into the Makeup tent.

CHAPTER ELEVEN

Shelley stood nervously outside the production office and looked up and down the hall for Pamela. Why was she always late for everything? she thought, annoyed. Shelley was just the opposite. She was always early — for dates, for dentist appointments, even for class. She thought briefly of her math test that was going on right that minute, and felt guilty.

Maybe she should have explained to Mr. Sutton that she just couldn't get to class that day, but what if he decided to report her to P.A.? He'd never understand that the movie had to come first. And neither would P.A., she thought grimly. Especially after her little pep talk in the assembly that morning. "Studies must come first, girls," she had said, and had flashed that no-nonsense stare. And of course, Alison would be just as bad. Shelley leaned against the wall and sighed. Nobody really understood how much *Midnight Whis-*

pers meant to her, she decided. No one except Pamela.

As if on cue, Pamela strolled up to her. "What's wrong? You look as if the world is going to come to an end in five minutes," she said wryly. Then she gave a bark of laughter. "I know who you remind me of — Susan Hayward in *I Want to Live*."

"I'm glad you're here," Shelley said nervously. "Did you talk to Yvonne?"

"Of course I did. I told you I would," Pamela answered calmly. She took out a compact and touched up her lip gloss. "Have you seen Carol around anywhere?"

"Carol Gate? I think she's inside." She pointed to the production office.

Pamela smiled at her. "Then what are we waiting for? Let's go. Yvonne gave her a ring this morning, and she promised to come up with something for you."

"Really! That's fantastic," Shelley said excitedly. "Do you think she will?" She felt on top of the world again. She had been right to trust Pamela after all.

"If she wants to work for Tony again, she will," Pamela said nastily. "We'll soon find out." She opened the door to the office without knocking, and spotted Carol. "Hi there," she said jauntily. "This is Shelley Hyde, your new star."

Shelley felt her face get crimson. Why did Pamela have to overplay everything? she wondered. All she wanted was a small part in the film. Any part!

"Hello, Pamela," Carol said smoothly. "I've been expecting you." She turned to Shelley and looked her up and down. "Hi, Shelley. I'm sorry that the part of Susan didn't work out for you." Shelley couldn't tell if she was saying it to be polite, or if she really meant it.

"Oh, that's all right. Like they say, that's show biz," Pamela answered for her. "The point is," she went on, "what can you do for Shelley now?" She peeled off her plum-colored suede coat, and sank into a chair, suddenly all business.

Carol smiled thinly at both of them. "Not a whole lot, I'm afraid. As you know, Pamela, most of the casting was done in L.A., and we only planned on picking up a few extras and stand-ins here in Massachusetts."

"Well, plans can change," Pamela said pleasantly. She stared steadily at Carol, obviously waiting for her to make the next move.

Carol shrugged and ran a hand through her short brown hair. "If you want, I can call Tracey in casting and line you up as an extra, Shelley. Or maybe a stand-in."

Pamela started to say something, but this time, Shelley jumped in first. "I know what an extra is, but what's a stand-in?"

"A nobody," Pamela said in a bored voice.

"It's not what I had in mind at all," she explained to Shelley.

Carol glared at her, and turned her attention to Shelley. "A stand-in is someone who literally 'stands in' during camera rehearsals for one of the principal actors, Shelley. Stand-ins never actually appear on camera, but they play an important part in the production."

"Yeah, they sure do," Pamela snorted. "They stand around freezing in the cold and rain while some dumb cameraman tries to get the angles and the lighting right. And in the meantime, the real actors are relaxing back in their trailers."

"What do you think, Shelley?" Carol asked, ignoring Pamela. "Do you think you'd be interested?" She tapped her pencil on her clipboard and glanced at her watch.

"Gee, I don't know," Shelley said hesitantly. "It doesn't sound like it's really acting. I mean, it sounds like anybody could do it," she added dispiritedly.

"They could!" Pamela hooted. "You could have a dummy, you know, a mannequin, standing out there, couldn't you, Carol? In fact, Foxfire would probably prefer it. They wouldn't have to feed it. Or pay it." She laughed uproariously at her own joke, and Carol's face tightened.

"Pamela," she said, after a moment, "I've told you and Shelley what my suggestions are. If you're not interested —"

"We're not," Pamela said, her voice suddenly cold. She stood up slowly, and nudged Shelley. "C'mon, Shel. We're wasting our time here."

"Uh, thank you for seeing me," Shelley muttered, embarrassed. She couldn't believe how rude Pamela was! Carol seemed really nice, and it wasn't her fault that nothing was available. In fact, come to think of it, it all went back to Pamela, she reminded herself. She was the main reason she had blown the audition!

As soon as they got outside, Pamela said furiously, "Wait till Yvonne hears about this. She'll hit the ceiling, she really will." She buttoned her coat, and pulled on some leather gloves. "I'll catch you later, Shel, okay? We can have dinner with Yvonne in her trailer, and figure out something else."

"Okay, thanks," Shelley told her. She felt very tired, and more let down than ever. The movie business was crazy! One minute you're in, then you're out. You're up, then you're down. None of it made any sense.

She stood outside the main building for a minute, wondering what to do next. Her eyes roamed over the campus, and she suddenly spied Faith in her bright red coat, hurrying along the icy walk. "Hey, Faith, wait up," she yelled. Faith stopped and turned and Shelley raced past the science building to catch up with her.

"What happened to you?" Faith said, a minute later. "You weren't in math class."

"I had too much to do," Shelley said quickly. "I'll tell you about it later. Where are you headed?" she said brightly. "I could use some company."

Faith gave her a funny look. "Are you sure you're okay?"

"Yes, I'm okay," Shelley said. She shrugged. "I guess I'm just feeling a little down. Can I tag along with you?"

"Sure, but I'm just going to try to get some shots on the set. Foxfire never got around to giving me permission, so it's like an undercover mission. Right now, they're filming a scene down at the birch grove, so I thought I'd try my luck there."

"Good, I'll come with you," Shelley said. *This may be the nearest I'll get to a movie set,* she thought, and felt depressed all over again.

"Casey's in this scene, I think," Faith said, as they hurried along the walk.

"Wonderful," Shelley said drily. Casey was an extra, Dana had a speaking part, and Faith was taking pictures. It was beginning to sound like everybody was connected in some way with the movie. Everybody but her.

The first person Shelley spotted on the set was Troy Adams. The second was Dana. "I can't believe she's in this scene," she muttered to Faith. "Just my luck."

Faith shrugged and groped in her pocket for some extra rolls of film. "I wish you two would settle whatever's going on between you," she said irritably. "I'm sick of being caught in the cross-fire." She paused and looked at Shelley. "Believe it or not, this movie has caused *me* a few problems, too. I just haven't bothered telling anyone about them."

Shelley didn't say anything for a minute, and then said guiltily, "I'm sorry, Faith. I guess I've been so disappointed at losing the part, I just haven't been thinking about anybody's else's problems. I'll try not to be such a drag, honest."

"Well, it would be nice not to have to live in an armed camp," Faith told her, with a smile. "If you and Dana could just declare some sort of truce in 407, I'd be grateful."

They were standing at the edge of a crowd of students watching the filming, and Faith decided that this would be a good time to take a few shots. She lifted her camera out of her coat as unobtrusively as possible and focused on a weary-looking cameraman who was reading a paperback novel between takes. She guessed at the exposure, quickly estimated the shutter speed, and took three shots in rapid succession. "I think I got it," she said in a low voice. The cameraman gave an enormous yawn on the last shot.

"You should get a shot of Troy," Shelley said softly. "Just look at him. Isn't he a dream?"

Faith followed her gaze to the edge of the

birch grove, where Troy Adams was standing next to a portable heater. He was rubbing his hands together and hopping on one foot. "I think I've got frostbite. You may have to amputate," he said jokingly to a sound technician. A production assistant threw a heavy blanket over his shoulders, and someone handed him a cup of steaming coffee.

"You're right, I've got to get a picture of that," Faith said impishly. Troy Adams, sex symbol and superstar, was squatting in front of the heater, munching doughnuts and laughing like a kid. When Dana walked by, he said to her playfully, "Hey, honey. Want to share my blanket?"

Faith and Shelley couldn't hear her reply, but Shelley's face tightened in a scowl. Dana had all the luck, she thought disgustedly. She should be the one on the set with Troy, acting with him, teasing him, sharing his blanket!

During the next hour, Faith took about a dozen shots of Troy, and the other actors. The filming moved at a snail's pace, and they didn't seem to accomplish very much. Troy had the opening line in the scene. As soon as the director yelled, "Places, everyone, and . . . action!" he was supposed to walk over to Dana and say: "Is it true what they say about sorority girls?" It looked easy enough, Faith thought, but they actually had to do seven or eight takes to get it right. The first few times, Troy's mike didn't work, and once he stepped on Dana's foot and she yelled. Another time, someone on the crew sneezed at a crucial moment, and got chewed out by the assistant director. Between each take, everyone stood around with chattering teeth, waiting for the mikes and cameras to be set up all over again.

It was almost impossible to tell what the scene was all about, and Faith wished that they'd take a break, so Dana could explain it to them. Shelley was watching the whole thing spellbound, and it was obvious from her expression that she wasn't impressed with Dana's acting skills.

"Did you see the way she delivered that line?" she whispered to Faith at one point. "She started talking before she even got up to him. She probably wasn't even on camera for half of her speech!"

"Well, maybe they told her to play it that way," Faith whispered back. She shook her head. It was obvious that Shelley was still tremendously jealous of Dana, and that the war was still on.

"Well, if they did, Albritton isn't much of a director," Shelley retorted. She started to say something else, when a really cute guy in a sheepskin jacket picked up a megaphone. "Okay everybody, take a ten-minute break. Maybe if we're lucky, we can wind this up before dinner."

A cheer went up from the cast, and everybody headed for the big silver catering truck that was parked at the entrance to the grove. Faith spotted Dana walking alone, and yelled to her.

Dana looked up, and Faith thought that her face clouded briefly when she saw Shelley, but she couldn't be sure. She recovered quickly, though, because she waved and came over.

"Hi," she said, and smiled briefly at them. "I didn't know you'd be here."

"We thought we'd ask you for an autograph," Shelley said. She meant it as a joke, but it came out as sarcastic, and Dana looked annoyed.

"Look, Shelley," she began, "are you still back on that kick?"

"Uh, I want to get a shot of you," Faith interjected quickly. The only way to ward off a fight between Dana and Shelley was to stay one step ahead of them, she decided. "How about if you just stand near one of the cameras? You can be studying your script, or something."

"Sure," Dana said shortly. She shot an angry look at Shelley and moved back onto the set with Faith. The less she talked to Shelley the better!

Watching Faith photograph Dana in her first movie was just too much for Shelley to take, and she wandered over to the catering truck. She was watching the actors line up for coffee and doughnuts, when someone interrupted her thoughts.

"Are you sure the coffee's worth waiting for?" The deep male voice came from behind her.

"The doughnuts are only good for one thing. Doorstops," the voice continued. "Or maybe paperweights."

Shelley giggled then, and forgot she was supposed to be depressed and bitter. "You could write a book, *A Hundred Uses for a Stale Doughnut* —" She turned around and was as stunned as if she had run into a brick wall. It was Troy Adams. He had gotten rid of the blanket, and looked really handsome in a tan parka with a fur-lined hood.

"We've met," he said politely. "You read with me one night at auditions."

"I . . . I know," Shelley gulped. "I'm surprised you'd remember me, though." Surprised was an understatement. Astounded would be a better word!

"Of course I'd remember such a beautiful girl," he said lightly. "And such a talented actress."

"Do you really think so?" Shelley blurted out. "Because I've started to think that maybe I can't act at all. My roommate, Dana, got the part, and she's never acted a day in her life."

"I can tell," Troy said, looking deep into Shelley's eyes. "She seems like a nice girl, but she just doesn't have it. Acting is something that's deep inside you, and if it's not there, it's not there. You're a million times more talented than she is," he said, lowering his voice.

"I'm glad you think so," Shelley managed to say. She was deliriously happy. "I just wish the director had thought so," she added.

"Oh, well, Tony's a great guy, but sometimes he's hard to figure out. The real secret with him is to overplay everything. Really ham it up. That's what he loves. Everybody in the business kids him about it." The line moved forward and Troy steered Shelley in front of him.

"So that's the secret," Shelley said slowly. Pamela had been a rat after all. Unless . . . she really hadn't known. "I wish I had known that before. Now it's too late."

"It's never too late for a gorgeous girl like you," Troy said. "Why don't you let me get you a cup of hot chocolate, and we'll try to figure something out?" He let his hand rest lightly on the collar of her coat, and she was so thrilled, she was afraid to move. She was almost afraid to breathe! Just a few minutes ago, she had been in the depths of despair, and now everything was working out. Pamela was right on one thing. Show business was really crazy.

CHAPTER TWELVE

When Shelley got to the dining hall a couple of hours later, she saw Faith sitting alone by the window, toying with her dinner. She took a quick look at the hot food counter — creamed cod was the special — and decided to stick to the salad bar. She was too excited to eat anyway. In fact, she was practically too excited to sit still!

"I gave up on you," Faith said, when Shelley finally slid into the seat next to her. "Even the beef stew got tired of waiting for you. I think it died." She dipped her spoon tentatively into a thick, gray stew, and swirled it around.

Shelley took one look and shuddered. "I'm really sorry," she said breathlessly. "You won't believe what happened. This has been the most wonderful afternoon of my whole life."

Faith stared at her in mock surprise. "Really? I never would have guessed it. The last time we spoke, you were ready to jump off a bridge."

"I know," Shelley giggled. "But isn't it funny how things can change?" She sighed, picked up her fork, and put it down again. "You know, Faith, things have a way of working out when you least expect them to, and — by the way, what are you doing?" she said suddenly. Faith was still prodding the congealed stew with her fork. "You're poking around that stew like you're hunting for buried treasure."

"I know," Faith said sheepishly. "I keep hoping I'll find something in there worth eating." She grinned and pushed the dish away.

"Oh, who can eat at a time like this?" Shelley said dramatically. "Don't you want to hear the most fantastic news of all time?"

"They've hired a new cook?" Faith said innocently. "This one could give me anorexia."

"No, silly." Shelley rolled her eyes. "I'm in *Midnight Whispers*! I got a part!"

She was grinning from ear to ear, and Faith started smiling, too. "That's super," she agreed. "How did it work out?"

"Troy Adams," Shelley said slowly. "He's the key to everything," she said dreamily. "He said I was a really gifted actress, and it was crazy that I couldn't work on the film with him."

"Uh-oh," Faith said quietly.

"What do you mean, 'uh-oh'?" Shelley demanded. "He's terrific. He managed to get me a part when no one else could."

"It sounds like the beginning of a giant, full-fledged crush, that's all," Faith said. "When you get that faraway look in your eyes, it means trouble," she said with a sigh.

"Not this time," Shelley said firmly. "He just admires me — as an actress, I mean." She nibbled at her salad.

"Shelley, he's a movie star," Faith reminded her. "He meets hundreds of girls — maybe thousands." *And he probably gives them all the same line*, she wanted to say.

"Well, what if he does?" Shelley said calmly. "He's going to help me, and that's what's important. In fact, he already has. My first scene is tomorrow. Can you believe it?" She grinned and hugged herself, her blue eyes bright with excitement.

"Tell me something about the character you play," Faith said. "Maybe I can put a little piece in the *Clarion* about you and Dana getting chosen for parts."

Shelley flushed and said quickly, "Well, I don't have a name, exactly."

"You don't have a name?"

"Well, I'm sort of an extra." She hesitated. "I'm one of the sorority girls. I know it's not the kind of part I had in mind originally, but Troy said that it's still a great stepping stone.

You know, onward and upward to better things. I want to make sure I get a principal role in the next movie I do."

"Being an extra will help you do all that?" Faith said incredulously.

"It's a start," Shelley told her. "After all, plenty of talent scouts and producers will see *Midnight Whispers*, Troy says. And when it comes time to cast for other movies, they'll remember me. If I make an impression on them," she added hastily.

"How can you make an impression if you're in a crowd scene?" Faith said dubiously.

"Well, honestly, Faith, I don't know exactly. I'm just telling you what Troy said." She was starting to feel annoyed at Faith. That was really crazy; Faith was on her side!

"Okay, okay," Faith relented. "I'm not an expert on the movie business. If you say that it will help you be a star someday, that's cool with me. I'm happy for you."

"I know you are." She didn't say anything for a minute, and then said hesitantly, "Where's Dana? I thought she'd be here by now."

"She's probably eating with the cast," Faith said lightly. "I doubt we'll even see her back at the room until late."

"I forgot about that," Shelley said, her spirits sinking. Of course, that's the way it would be from now on. Dana would get to have all her meals with the cast, because she had a real speaking part. The extras would be shuffled off to separate tables from the stars — if they got invited to eat at all! It was a disgusting situation. And there was absolutely nothing she could do about it. Except make the most of her tiny part, and her connection with Troy Adams.

Faith was staring at her and saying something, and she forced her mind back to the present. "Listen, Shel, are you almost ready to go back to the room? I don't know about you, but I've got a ton of homework waiting for me. I'll wait for you while you finish your salad, though."

"Oh, no, I'm ready to go. It's hard to get interested in wilted lettuce," she said, picking up her tray. She had barely touched her food, but it didn't really matter. There was only one thing in the world she was interested in, and at that very moment, he was probably with Dana Morrison!

If someone had told Dana that acting was such hard work, she never would have believed them. She stared at the other actors who were laughing and talking at the long metal table in the dining tent. They had finally called a break for dinner at seven o'clock, but she was so tired, she felt like it was midnight!

She wondered why she was so wiped out. Her lines were simple enough, but there were endless takes and retakes, and she'd spent a lot of time waiting around in the cold. *I guess it's worth it, though,* she decided, staring at Peter. He was sitting next to her, cheerfully wolfing down a giant dish of lasagna.

When he felt her eyes on him, he turned and grinned. "All set for another four hours?"

"Another four hours?" He had to be kidding! She could barely lift her fork.

"Sure," he said, reaching for a basket of French bread. "The night's still young, you know. We usually break at midnight. Although now that I think of it, we're moving on to the scene on the library steps. I don't think you're in that one. Unless you'd like to stick around and watch," he offered. "Maybe we could go into Greenleaf or something, when we finish shooting."

"At midnight?" she nearly blurted out. Alison would have a fit. Plus she was exhausted, and she had homework to do. Dana didn't want to sound like a baby with a curfew, though, so she just laughed and said, "I hate to tell you, Peter, but Greenleaf takes in the sidewalks at nine."

"Oh, too bad," he said casually. He polished off an enormous piece of apple pie and looked at his watch. "Well, at least let me walk you back to your dorm," he said. "When you're finished eating, I mean." He stood up and shrugged into his parka.

"Sure, I'm ready," she said, pushing back her chair. She had barely touched her dinner, but she could always grab something out of the machine later.

"Do you want the grand tour or the three-minute one?" Dana asked him, as they walked. They had left the dining tent and were hurrying past the library. "Although it's pretty hard to tell everything about Canby Hall in three minutes," she began. "You see, Horace Canby was —"

She never got any further because the next thing she knew, Peter had stopped, right in the middle of the icy walk, and kissed her! She was so surprised, she nearly toppled over.

"Peter," she began. "That's a no-no around here," she said breathlessly. She couldn't believe that he was kissing her right in the middle of campus.

"What is?" he said blankly. He pulled back to look at her, but kept his arms encircling her waist.

"This," she said and started to giggle. "Kissing." She gently pulled away from him and started back down the walk. "We can hold hands, though," she told him.

"Wonderful," he said sarcastically. "I love holding hands. You know, I think this school is right out of the Middle Ages," he added glumly.

Dana smiled. "It's not that bad. They're just really strict on stuff like that. People do kiss, of course, but they're usually more . . . discreet about it." They were almost back at

Baker House, and Dana found herself wishing she could have more time with him. "This is my dorm," she said reluctantly.

"Ah, the spot where we part company," he said with a smile. "Unless you've changed your mind about meeting me later?"

She shook her head. "I really can't." She started up the stairs and stopped. "Will I see you tomorrow?" He was still holding her hand.

"Unless you plan on working the sound boom yourself, you will," he laughed. "I think we're doing another outdoor scene tomorrow — the maple grove, probably. You can check with Carol first thing in the morning. We've got a six-thirty call, but you probably don't have to check in till later."

"I hope not." Dana felt herself smiling at him. He was so good-looking, standing on the step below her, looking at her with those marvelous eyes. *He's a thousand times more attractive than Troy Adams,* she caught herself thinking. Peter could be a movie star himself someday. "Well," she said hesitantly, "thanks for everything . . . the dinner. . . ."

"That's not the way to say good-night," Peter said softly. In one swift movement, he had his arms around her, and kissed her firmly on the lips. "That's more like it." He chuckled and headed down the steps. "Sweet dreams," he said softly.

I'm sure they will be, Dana said silently.

She practically floated up the stairs to 407, and wondered how she'd ever be able to work on her history term paper. All she wanted to do was relive every single moment she had spent with Peter.

"You got a call from the Urban Cowboy," Faith greeted her. "He said to please call him back, no matter how late it is." She and Shelley were sprawled on the floor mattresses, surrounded by a sea of books and papers.

Dana peeled off her poncho and stared at herself in the mirror. She looked flushed, excited. "You mean Randy?" she said slowly. She had completely forgotten about him, and felt a twinge of guilt. "I'll call him later," she told Faith, who had already gone back to her book. She stood in front of the mirror, smiling a little, remembering Peter's kiss. Kisses, she corrected herself. One on the walk, and one on the steps. She started to giggle, and Shelley gave her a funny look.

"Why don't you let us in on the joke?" she said coolly. "We could use a few laughs around here." She put down her pen and studied Dana.

"Oh, it's nothing," Dana said quickly. "Just something someone said on the set today. You'd have to be there to really, uh . . . appreciate it." She shot a worried look at Shelley. That hadn't been the most tactful thing in the world to say!

Shelley seemed unconcerned, though, and

slid off the mattress to grab a diet drink.
"Well, as a mater of fact, I will be on the
set," she said. "As of tomorrow."

"You got a part? That's terrific!" Dana was
delighted. If Shelley got a part, everything
would be okay, and there would be an end to
this crazy rivalry.

Her hopes were dashed, though, because
after a pause, Shelley said, "It's nothing like
your part, of course. I'm an extra." She took a
swig of diet cola and settled back down on the
mattress. "Just like Casey. I'll be in the sorority scene, and maybe in a couple of the other
scenes."

"I'm really happy to hear it," Dana said.

"So am I," Faith said fervently. "In fact,
why don't we make a toast?" She handed
Dana a glass and raised her own. "To *Midnight Whispers*." She paused, as Dana and
Shelley raised their glasses. "May it be a big
success. . . ."

"And may we all get what we want out of
it," Shelley finished for her. As they touched
glasses, Faith noticed that Dana was smiling,
but Shelley's mouth was drawn in a tight
line, and she had a grimly determined look
on her face. The competition wasn't over,
she thought. Not by a long shot.

Faith woke up early the next morning, and
decided to put Plan B into action. She had already accomplished Plan A — taking informal
shots of the cast and crew — but now she had

a bigger target. She wanted to get some candid shots of the stars. It was riskier, she knew, because big stars, like Yvonne, absolutely refused to have their picture taken. Unless it was by someone really famous, who made them look twenty years younger, Faith thought wryly. She had seen some of Yvonne's publicity shots, and they made her look like Pamela's sister.

Her first stop was the production office, where she checked the call-board. Yvonne had an eight-thirty call for a scene in the lounge at Addison House, one of three dorms at Canby Hall. Perfect! She hurried across the campus, and ducked into the lounge just as Yvonne was making her grand entrance. Except it wasn't the elegant, gracious Yvonne who had swept into Baker House a week ago — it was a furious woman with the strangest hairdo Faith had ever seen.

"Where is Shirley!" Yvonne shouted. "Look at this mess! I look like a punk rock star." It was true. Her blonde hair was standing all over her head in spikes, and Faith had to resist the urge to giggle.

A wardrobe woman trailed after her with a pin cushion. "I still think that hemline's uneven, Miss Young," she said worriedly.

"Well, get it right!" Yvonne shouted at her. "Honestly! Can't anybody do anything right around here? First the hair, and now the clothes. And Makeup! Where is Makeup?"

"Right here, Miss Young," Alex said

mildly. He must be used to stars having temper tantrums, Faith decided, because he seemed to ignore the outburst. He took out a giant powder puff and started working on Yvonne's face. "We thought you'd be in the Makeup tent this morning," he explained.

"I never go to Makeup," Yvonne said coldly. "They come to me. In fact, this is the first time that I haven't brought my own makeup woman with me. The producer was too cheap to allow it," she said loudly.

Everyone was listening to Yvonne, spellbound, and no one noticed when Faith surreptitiously started snapping some pictures. She got some wonderful ones, she thought. Yvonne shouting at the wardrobe lady, Yvonne frowning at Alex, Yvonne pushing her way imperiously through a crowd of extras. She could hardly wait to get back to the room to develop them. They'd make a fantastic addition to her portfolio. And she knew exactly what she'd call the whole collection. "*Midnight Whispers*: An Inside Look." It would be dynamite!

CHAPTER THIRTEEN

The next few days flew by, and by the following Wednesday, Dana was on a permanent high. Everything was working out perfectly! She spent her mornings in class, her afternoons on the set, and she had dinner with the cast and crew — including Peter — every single night. She was tired most of the time, and rarely got to bed before midnight, but that was a small price to pay for having such an exciting time. After all, as Alison always said, "anything worth doing in life takes a lot of hard work." Well, she was working harder than she ever had, and was loving every minute of it!

At three-thirty that day, she bundled up in a navy pea coat and was taking the Baker House stairs two at a time, when she ran into Faith on the fourth floor landing.

"You've got a visitor," Faith told her absently. For a minute, it didn't sink in. Dana had raced back to Baker House to change clothes, and her mind was on the next scene. She had exactly fifteen minutes to make it to the maple grove.

"What did you say?" she asked breathlessly. She was mentally going over her lines. First the "spirit" would make a brief appearance, and then Dana would look terrified, turn, and —

"Your boyfriend's here," Faith said, knowingly. "And if you don't want him, there are some cute freshmen hanging around who look like they're ready to pounce on him."

What was Peter doing at Baker House? Dana wondered. He should be in the maple grove right this minute, setting up the mikes and checking the equipment. "Thanks," she muttered briefly. She shook her head and hurried past Faith.

When she got to the bottom of the stairs, the mystery was solved. Her "boyfriend" was waiting for her, all right. Except it wasn't Peter.

It was Randy.

Dana's heart sank. She had completely forgotten to return his call! He must think she was terrible. Well, she thought, taking a deep breath, there was nothing to do but make a quick explanation and hope for the best.

"Hi, Randy," she said brightly. "This is a nice surprise."

"Is it?" he said, giving her an ironic grin. "I wasn't sure if you'd be glad to see me or not."

"Randy, that's crazy!" she blurted out. "I'm always glad to see you." He gave her a funny look, and she wondered if she was overplaying it. Whenever she felt guilty or defensive about anything, she tended to go overboard in the opposite direction.

"Well, when I didn't hear from you —" he began.

"Randy, I want to explain about that," she said quickly, "but why don't we go outside where we can . . . uh, talk." A few girls were giving them curious stares, and Dana linked her arm through Randy's and steered him through the lounge.

The bright sunlight hit her as soon as they stepped out on the porch, and Dana reached for her sunglasses.

"Oh, no," Randy moaned. "She's gone Hollywood already."

"I have not," Dana retorted. "The glare of the sun on the snow makes my eyes sting."

"Sure," he said, still teasing. "You know, you really look cute in those aviator glasses," he admitted. "Like a beautiful pilot." Dana looked at him and felt relieved. Maybe he wasn't mad after all. They headed across the campus, and after a moment, he said, "I'll make it easy for you. You didn't call me back the other night, because you've been busy."

"Yes, I really have," she said gratefully. "I've got the craziest schedule you can imagine, Randy, but everything is so . . . wonderful. This has been the most exciting time of my whole life." He reached for her mittened hand and she smiled up at him. He was so cute! She could see why the girls in the lounge were dying to meet him. "You do understand, don't you?"

"I guess so," he replied. "I've got to confess, I'll be glad when this movie business is over, though. I suppose it's sort of a once-in-a-lifetime thing for you."

"That's right," Dana said earnestly. "I'll never have this chance again. I still can't believe I'm getting the chance to do it right now." She glanced at her watch. "We have to head for the maple grove," she added. "That's where my next scene is."

Randy nodded, and slipped his arm around her waist. "So tell me," he said after a minute, "what do you like best about the movie business?"

She felt like saying the first thing that popped into her head, but she didn't dare. *Peter*, she said silently. *Peter Marks is the main attraction.* "I like the idea of putting myself on the line," she said finally. She knew that was something he could relate to. "Of doing something that I thought I couldn't do."

"I can understand that," Randy said solemnly. "That's the way I felt when I first learned to break a pony. I was scared to death the first time, but I really felt like I had accomplished something when it was over."

Dana had to smile at the comparison.

"Then you can understand how much this means to me," she said gently. She felt like a hypocrite, but what else could she do? She obviously couldn't tell him about Peter.

"I can," he said, giving her hand a squeeze. "But don't blame me if I want my girl back, okay?"

She nodded and didn't say anything. They were at the maple grove, and the last thing in the world she wanted was a confrontation between Peter and Randy. Casey and Shelley were standing at the edge of the grove, and they turned and waved when they spotted her. "Uh, this is where I'm supposed to go," she said hesitantly. "We'll be filming for two or three hours at least," she added.

He didn't take the hint. "Oh, well, I'm not doing anything this afternoon," Randy said cheerfully. "I wouldn't mind hanging around and seeing what this movie business is all about."

"You can't!" Dana said it more sharply than she intended, and Randy looked at her, puzzled. "I mean," she added quickly, "they don't allow visitors on the set. They're awfully strict about stuff like that." She smiled to show that she, personally, thought the rule was dreadfully unfair, and that she'd be thrilled if he could stay.

Randy wasn't convinced. "But what are all these people doing here?" he said, peering at the crowd. "It looks to me like they're just standing around watching."

"Those are . . . extras," she said, improvising quickly. "You see, we're doing a crowd scene, and they're all going to be part of it."

"Oh." He shrugged and stuffed his hands in his pockets. "Well, maybe I better be going then. I don't want to be in your way."

"It's nothing like that," she said lamely. "It's just that I really have to get to work in a couple of minutes."

As if on cue, a voice rang out, "Scene sixteen! Tommy Mason, Adrienne Hardy, and Susan Blake, report to the set please."

"That's me," Dana said. Randy looked puzzled. "Susan Blake — that's my character." She tried to give him a reassuring smile to show she really cared, but she wished he'd hurry up and leave!

"Oh," Randy said again. "So I guess I better shove off." He tried a little smile, but Dana could tell his heart wasn't in it. "I guess there's no point in trying to pin you down for a date this weekend, is there? There's supposed to be a great old movie playing at the Rialto this Saturday night." He paused and looked at her very seriously. "Although come to think of it, watching a movie couldn't compare to starring in one yourself, could it?" He gave a short laugh.

"Randy," she began, "I'm hardly a star, and anyway, you know I'd love to see you —" She broke off when she saw Peter heading in their direction.

"Actors for scene sixteen, where are you?" The voice on the megaphone had a decidedly impatient edge to it this time.

"I've really got to go." Dana shrugged helplessly.

"That's okay. You can't keep your public waiting," Randy said lightly. "Don't worry about it. Give me a ring if you get a chance." He vanished into the crowd, just as Peter appeared by her side. Another two seconds and she would have had to introduce them. Talk about close encounters! She'd never make it as a spy, she decided. This cloak-and-dagger stuff was making her so nervous, she had already forgotten her lines.

"Hi, beautiful." Peter tugged playfully on her scarf and gave her that special smile. Whenever he looked at her that way, all the lights and cameras and people disappeared, and she felt like it was just the two of them all alone on a desert island. She was sure he felt that way, too. "All set to live a night of stark terror?"

"I hope so. This is the scene where the spirit spoils the party, isn't it?"

"It sure is. We've been stocking up on cranberry juice all day."

"Cranberry juice?" They had moved toward the set, and he began adjusting a boom mike.

"It makes great blood."

"Oh." Dana tried not to shudder. She had

forgotten that whenever the spirit was out of sorts, it went on a rampage and polished off a few dozen people.

"Don't worry, it doesn't get Susan in this scene," Peter said, as if he could read her thoughts. "Just try to stay out of the way, and you won't get splashed. Have you got your script handy?" He finished whatever he was doing with the mike, and walked over to her.

He was standing very close to her as she dug the wrinkled sheets out of her pocket. "Here it is," she said, a little nervously. "I've only got three lines, and the rest is just a lot of screaming." She had underlined all her dialogue with magic marker so she could spot it instantly.

"Mmm-hmm," Peter said. "I see what you mean." He let his hand rest very gently on the bare curve of her neck, the spot right between her coat and her scarf. Suddenly he was looking at her, not the script, and he didn't seem in any hurry to move off.

"Peter, I hate to break this up, but the mike's dead," someone said sarcastically. "Check the connections, will you?"

"Be right there," Peter called back. "See you later, Dana," he whispered. He quickly covered the set with his long, graceful strides, and Dana could hardly take her eyes off him. She felt a little guilty over the way she had treated Randy — after all, they had been friends for a long time — but Peter was somethink else. He was fantastic. There was no one to compare with him. She sighed and looked at her crumpled script. Her lines were silly, ridiculous. It didn't matter. She smiled and glanced at her watch. Only four hours till dinner with Peter!

Shelley watched Dana the whole time she was talking to Peter, and felt insanely jealous. Not of Peter, of course. Who could look at Peter when Troy Adams was around! She was jealous because Dana had a speaking part, and she didn't.

She absolutely hated being an extra, she decided. When Troy had first suggested it, she had thought it was a pretty good idea, but it wasn't working out at all like she had planned. In the first place, extras were nobodies — less than second-class citizens. There was nothing unique or special about them — they were faceless, like cattle. Yes, that was it exactly, she decided. They were like a herd of cattle.

And worst of all, they weren't allowed to mingle with the stars. If she had hoped to see much of Troy on the set, she was kidding herself. He stayed in his trailer between takes, while she stood shivering in a pile of slush! And extras were't even invited to eat with other actors. It was all just too unfair. She was feeling immensely sorry for herself when a deep male voice broke into her thoughts.

"Things can't be that bad, can they? Or does the spirit get you in this scene?"

Troy! She was instantly giddy with happiness. She didn't want him to see how depressed she was, so she said lightly, "Everything's about a hundred percent better now that you're here."

"Just a hundred?" He pretended to frown. "I usually make people feel a thousand percent better."

She laughed. He was so adorable. If anyone else said that, she would have thought he was unbearably conceited, but Troy had a way of turning everything into a joke.

"What are you doing after the filming tonight?" he said suddenly.

"Tonight?" She hesitated. She was supposed to meet Tom in Greenleaf for a quick hamburger, and then she had promised herself she would hit the books.

"Yes, tonight," he said patiently. He made a howling noise. "You know, about seven o'clock when the sun goes down, and all the werewolves come out."

"Nothing," she said quickly. "Nothing at all." She'd be darned if she was going to turn him down. After all, she had her whole life to learn the subjunctive, didn't she? How many evenings would she have to spend with a movie star!

"Then let's go to dinner together. Is there anyplace here that makes good hamburgers?

They're my passion in life. One of my passions," he teased.

"There's . . . there's a place in Greenleaf," she gulped.

"Fine. Okay, here's what we'll do. Why don't you meet me in my trailer — it's that silver-and-blue one — around six-thirty, and we'll take it from there."

"That would be wonderful." She could hardly get the words out.

"Well, I don't know about wonderful," he said with a laugh. "But I've got to make you feel nine hundred percent better, remember?"

"Right!"

"See you then, honey," he told her, just as someone yelled for him to be on the set.

Honey! He called her honey? She took back everything she had said about being an extra. *Midnight Whispers* was the most fantastic thing in the world to ever happen to her.

She was in a happy daze when Pamela walked up to her. "I saw you talking to Troy," she said shortly. "How come you — I mean, how did you happen to, uh . . . meet him?"

"I met him the other day when I was watching the filming," Shelley said. She was trying to peer around Pamela to get another glimpse of him.

"And —" Pamela's voice was hard, but Shelley was too excited to worry about it.

"And he remembered me from the audition. He even offered to help me, and that's

how I got a part. As an extra," she explained.
She was going to say that Troy thought she
was a much better actress than Dana, but
decided against it. After all, Dana was her
friend, and her roommate. It wasn't her fault
that she couldn't act.

"That's interesting," Pamela said coolly.
"An extra? I didn't think that was quite what
you had in mind." A thin smile curled the
corners of her lips.

"Well, it wasn't," Shelley said defensively.
"But I'll still get a chance to be on the set,
and who knows? Maybe some day, a director
will see the movie, and ask for me."

"I can't believe this," Pamela said. She
brushed her blonde hair out of her eyes. She
was wearing a black turtleneck sweater and
a bright red ski jacket, and looked sensational.
"Shel, if you talk like that, people will think
you just fell off a turnip truck. No one dis-
covers extras. As far as directors are concerned,
they don't even exist."

"Well, there weren't any speaking parts
left," Shelley said, turning to her. "You heard
what Carol Gate said. It was either this or
nothing." She couldn't understand why
Pamela was knocking everything she was
doing.

"Whatever you say," Pamela said nastily. "I
figured you weren't interested in a part anymore, since you never got back in touch with
me."

"Of course I was interested," Shelley said

indignantly. "But there was nothing anybody could do."

Pamela inspected her long, perfect, magenta nails. "There's always something someone can do," she said sweetly.

"Adrienne Hardy," a voice barked. "Come to the set immediately! We're doing scene sixteen."

"Uh-oh," Pamela said. "That's my cue."

"You're Adrienne Hardy?" Shelley was astonished. "I thought there weren't any parts left."

"They wrote one in for me." She gave Shelley a devastatingly sweet smile and walked away.

CHAPTER FOURTEEN

At six-twenty-five that night, a very nervous Shelley hesitated outside the sleek silver-and-blue trailer. She looked at her watch, urging the hands forward. She was a little early — should she wait? Should she go in? He had said six-thirty, but —

She didn't have to make a decision after all, because suddenly the door to the trailer opened, and a giggling girl emerged. She was beautiful, about twenty, and Shelley recognized her as one of the Foxfire crew. A script girl, whatever that was.

She stared briefly at Shelley, and then stuck her head back inside the trailer. "See you later, Troy," she said, and then gave a husky laugh. She bounced down the steps, and a moment later, Troy's muscular frame filled the doorway.

"Hey, at least close the door. It's freezing —" He stopped when he saw Shelley and grinned at her. "Hi, Shelley, come on in. I'll just grab a jacket and we can go."

"Thank you," she said primly, and stepped inside. She had daydreamed about what Troy's trailer would look like, but it was nothing like she had imagined. She had expected a wall-to-wall stereo system, elaborate furniture, and dozens of framed pictures of movie stars.

Instead, she found herself standing in the middle of a small, cramped trailer that was furnished in what Dana would call Modern Mediocre. Formica tables and oily leatherette chairs were grouped on a dingy linoleum floor. A battered black-and-white television was tuned to a quiz show, and Troy stared at it for a moment and then switched it off. He shrugged into a heavy parka and stopped as if he had suddenly thought of something.

"Hey, we'll need to call a cab," he said. "I don't have a car up here."

"We can walk," Shelley laughed. "It's only a mile into town."

"Walk?" Troy looked at her as if she was out of her mind.

"Everybody walks to Greenleaf," she told him. "We can be there in fifteen minutes." She grinned impishly at him. "You had to walk through fifteen miles of burning sand in your last movie, didn't you? In bare feet! And remember in *Desert Games* when you had to climb down that sixty-foot wall of solid rock —"

Troy laughed and threw his arm around her. "Okay, you made your point. We'll walk into town. But I'll let you in on a little secret of the movie business, honey. I never walk unless I get paid for it. I figure that's what we have stunt men for."

"So this is beautiful downtown Greenleaf," Troy said later when they were settled at a corner table in Pizza Pete's. Luckily there wasn't much business on a weeknight. Shelley didn't have to share Troy with a horde of autograph seekers. "Not exactly one of the country's hot spots, is it?"

"Well, it's not bad," Shelley said defensively. If Troy thought Greenleaf was a hick town, what would he think of her hometown — Pine Bluff, Iowa? Even Dana made jokes about it, and called it Pine Barf. "There's a movie theater, and some shops, and someday, they'll probably build a mall here."

Troy stared out the window at the snow-covered streets, and said feelingly, "It would drive me nuts to live in a place like this. Absolutely crazy. I like a lot of noise and lights and people. Excitement." He looked at her. "You'd love L.A., Shelley. I bet you've never been there."

She started to tell him that she'd never been *anywhere*, and stopped just in time. He already thought she was hopelessly naive. "I've never been out West," she said slowly. "I've been to Washington, D.C., though," she said, remembering the time she and Dana had visited Faith and her family. "It was wonderful. We went to the Smithsonian museums, and we saw Pennsylvania Avenue. . . ."

"You should see Sunset Strip," Troy told her, looking directly into her eyes. "It's wild. You can drive up and down the Strip in a convertible on a Saturday night, and you can see anything. And I mean anything." He shook his head and laughed. "It's like something out of a movie, except it's real life. And there's Rodeo Drive. I guess you've heard about that."

"It's where all the fancy shops are," Shelley said promptly. She had heard all about Rodeo Drive from Pamela. According to Pamela, there were only three places in the world to buy clothes — New York, Paris, and Rodeo Drive.

"Yeah, you can find anything you want there. They have everything from solid gold fountain pens to emerald rings the size of robins' eggs." He paused while the waitress put down the cheeseburger platter. She stared at him with open-mouthed admiration, and he gave her a good-natured grin.

"Is there anything else you need, Mr. Adams?" she said blushingly.

"No, we're fine," Shelley said crisply. She could hardly wait for the girl to leave. She didn't want to waste a precious minute of the time they had together.

"Maybe you'll get out there someday,"

Troy said, when the waitress reluctantly left them.

"To L.A.? I don't think so," Shelley said sadly. "Once school is over, I'll go back to Iowa for the summer." Even as she said it, she realized that she was dreading it. Troy was right. Small towns were hopelessly dull, and Pine Bluff was really the pits.

"That's too bad," Troy said sympathetically. "You know, this is crazy, but I wish you could get out to L.A. this month with us." He reached for the catsup and said casually, "I guess you've heard of Stevens Productions, haven't you?"

Shelley nodded. "They do all those action-adventure movies, don't they?"

"Yeah," he said with a laugh. "None of them even have a plot, but they give a lot of work to the stunt men. Stevens is shooting a new one in South America, and they're casting for it in a couple of weeks. I've got the second lead in it," he added modestly.

"You're going to be in it?" Shelley gulped.

"I play a journalist who's on the trail of some hidden treasure." He stopped and stared into space. "I think it will involve about four months of shooting, and most of it will be in the jungle. I know the sequence on the Amazon will take at least three weeks. It should be fun, though. At least it will be warm," he said with a laugh.

"It sounds very interesting," she said politely. She wondered why he was bothering to tell her so much about the movie. It was kind of a kick to have inside information, though, and she'd have some good stories to share with the girls in 407.

"So what do you think?" he said suddenly. His piercing eyes went right through her. "Are you interested?"

Her mind was a blank. "What do you mean?" She smiled uncertainly at him.

"Do you want to be in the flick?" He pushed the dish of French fries toward her, but she was paralyzed.

"Me?" Her voice came out in a whisper. "I could . . . get a part in the movie with you?" Her mind had absolutely screeched to a halt, but somehow she forced the words out. She must have misunderstood him. That was the only possible explanation.

"Why not?" he said lazily. "They shoot five days a week, so we could even do some sight-seeing. Maybe we could take some side trips on weekends. I've always wanted to fly down to Rio, haven't you?"

She hadn't misunderstood him. He actually wanted her to be in a movie with him! Her heart was pounding, but she tried to stay calm, so she could ask the right questions. She had never — never! — expected anything like this.

"Troy," she said slowly, "how could it work out? Do you think I'd really have a chance of getting a part? Wouldn't I have to get an agent and audition?"

"Not necessarily." He glanced at the menu. "Say, are you still hungry? I feel like some pie. Or maybe some ice cream."

"No, nothing, thanks." She wished he'd keep his mind on the movie. Her whole career was at stake, and he was worrying about his stomach! "About the movie," she prompted him.

He tore his attention away from a full-color picture of a hot fudge sundae and looked at her. "Oh yeah. Well, I'll tell you something, Shelley. I never go through the usual channels. I try to keep my life as simple as possible." He smiled at her, and suddenly it all seemed so easy. "Once you get out to L.A., I can introduce you to my agent, and he can set up the rest. But you'll have to come out to the Coast with us. It's not exactly the kind of thing you can do long distance."

"No, of course not. I understand that." She hesitated. "Tell me, Troy, what kind of part do you think I could get?" *I don't want to be an extra,* she pleaded silently.

"A good part," he said, surprised. "You know, one of the principal roles. I'll have to look at the script again, but as far as I can remember, there's a part you'd be perfect for. The character's name is Maria, and she's my sidekick." He laughed. "You wouldn't have to worry about getting hurt, either. We'd make sure that they got you a double to do all the stunts. All you'd have to do is know your lines and look beautiful. And for you, that would be a snap. You're a knockout." He smiled reassuringly at her.

Shelley didn't know what to say. It sounded so incredible — like a dream, a fantasy. "But it would be kind of complicated, wouldn't it?" she said softly. She was afraid that if she spoke too loudly, she'd break the spell she was under.

"Not unless you make it that way, Shelley," Troy said. "It's really very simple. Just fly back out to L.A. with us when we finish up here, and I'll make sure you meet the right people. That's the name of the game, honey. The right connections." He stood up and reached for the check.

The right connections, Shelley repeated to herself. He was absolutely right. All it took was enough courage to follow through on what you really want. And she was sure she had it.

When she got back to Baker House that night, Alison caught up with her on the stairs. "Have a minute, Shelley?" Alison's smile was friendly enough, but there was a cool note in her voice that wasn't lost on Shelley.

"Sure, what's up?"

"We can't talk here," Alison said quickly. "Come on up to my room." They walked up to Alison's apartment on the top floor, and Alison closed the door and took a deep breath. "Okay, you're not going to like this, so you might as well settle down with a snack." She opened two cans of diet soda and handed one to Shelley before she curled up on an over-stuffed chair. There was a plate of oatmeal cookies on the coffee table, but Shelley couldn't have eaten one to save her life.

"I don't think I like it already," Shelley said nervously. Alison had her "I-really-mean-business" look, and Shelley wondered what she had done.

"I'm not crazy over it myself, Shelley." Alison made a face, but Shelley couldn't tell if it was at her or at the diet drink. She was wearing a long, hand-printed Indian skirt and she tucked her legs under her. "And you know that I respect your privacy, and have faith in your judgment. Okay, now that I've said all that —"

"You're going to give me the bad news," Shelley interjected.

"Right. I'm very worried about you." She paused. "You've always been a good student, outside of French," Alison smiled. "I've always gotten good reports from your teachers. Now you're suddenly slipping."

"I still keep up," Shelley protested.

"Barely," Alison said flatly. "You failed your last math exam."

"Math just isn't my strong point," Shelley muttered.

Alison waved a pile of pink slips. "Neither is chemistry or English, according to these." She leaned forward. "Shelley, what's wrong?

Faith tells me you're barely going to class anymore."

"Faith told you that?" Shelley was furious. Who would think that Faith would turn out to be a rat! "Why didn't she mind her own business?"

"Because she's concerned about you," Alison said calmly. "If you saw her headed for trouble, wouldn't you do something to help her?"

"I suppose so." She picked up one of Alison's embroidered pillows and hugged it to her chest. "But Faith has nothing to worry about. And neither do you," she said quickly. "I've just had a lot on my mind lately."

"*Midnight Whispers.*"

"That's right. It was so important to me to get a part, I admit that I . . . put that ahead of my studies." She suddenly thought of a way out. "But don't you see? Now that I've actually got a part in the movie, everything's back to normal." She smiled. "I'll work hard, and never be late to class, and I'll be the old Shelley you know and love."

Alison laughed. "Well, I'd like to believe that. Are you sure that's all there is to it?" The relief in her voice was obvious. "You know I hate to have to check up on you like the Gestapo."

"That's all there is to it." Shelley stood up. "Now, if there isn't anything else, I've got to hit the books."

"Wait, there is one thing," Alison said. "It must be a mix-up, but Tom came by to pick you up. Something about having dinner at Pizza Pete's?"

Tom! She had completely forgotten about him. There was no sense in tipping off Alison, though. "Oh, honestly, that was for tomorrow night. He's hopeless about dates. I'll call him and straighten things out."

"And you'll really study and get back in the swing of things?"

"I'll be a grind," Shelley promised her. On the way down to 407, she had to smile. Alison really shouldn't worry about her grades, she thought. After all, she wouldn't even be at Canby Hall that much longer. She'd be in L.A., and then South America. With Troy Adams. Starring in her first feature film!

When Shelley got back to 407, she didn't let on that she had seen Alison. "Hi, gang," she said cheerfully. "What's everybody up to?"

Dana spoke up first. "I'm trying to unravel the mysteries of modern math, and Faith is — what are you doing, Faith?"

Faith was on her hands and knees on the floor, shuffling through dozens of black-and-white photos. "I'm going crazy, that's what. I can't decide what to throw away and what to keep."

Shelley knelt down next to her. She picked

up the shots Faith had taken in the maple grove and the makeup tent and looked through them. "They all look good to me."

"You've got to be selective, Shelley. At least that's what they taught us in photography. The trouble is, I like them all."

"I know someone who wouldn't like this one," Shelley laughed. She picked up a picture of Yvonne. "In fact, you better be careful with that camera. Pamela asked me a couple of times what you were doing. I mumbled something about a school project, but I don't think she was convinced."

Shelley looked at the picture again. It was taken in the harsh morning light, and it caught Yvonne with a scowl on her face. A worried-looking wardrobe mistress was holding up a dress for her inspection, while a makeup man and hairdresser hovered nearby. "She looks like she's saying, 'Off with their heads.'"

Faith laughed, too. "Lady Yvonne holding court. No, I don't think she'll want to use this on her Christmas cards. Don't worry, she'll never see it." She put the shot of Yvonne in the pile she wanted to keep. "It's definitely going in the portfolio, though. Even if I never show these in an exhibit, I want to have a record of *Midnight Whispers*. That's what photography is all about anyway. Memories."

Dana smiled absently. *As if I needed a picture to remember what it was like being in this movie,* she thought. Or meeting Peter. Who could forget a man like him? Even Pamela had noticed him, and she was the type who'd yawn if Rick Springfield showed up in the lounge. It's funny, but she had noticed Pamela talking to him on the set that day. She'd have to remember to ask him what it was about. . . .

"I hate to break this up, but it's getting late," Faith said. "And even though Alison's cool, if she sees a light under the door at this hour. . . ."

"You're right," Shelley said. She yawned and stretched. "Everybody needs to hit the sack." She looked at her math book, still unopened on her night table. It was much too late to study now. Anyway, she had some serious thinking to do. And serious planning. Going to L.A. with Troy was a very big step to take. It was wonderful, and exciting, and she knew it was all going to work out. But deep down, she had a nagging feeling in her stomach and a quivery feeling in her legs. She knew what it was.

Deep down, she was very scared.

CHAPTER FIFTEEN

The next couple of weeks were busy ones for the girls in 407, and especially for Dana, since she was the one who was the most involved with *Midnight Whispers*. One bright Saturday morning, she was yawning and stomping her feet in front of the science building, while the crew set up a scene. It was bitterly cold, and she was dying for a cup of coffee, but the catering truck was nowhere in sight.

Dana still couldn't get used to the "hurry-up-and-wait" part of movie-making. Sometimes she'd stand around the set for six hours at a stretch, and all they'd shoot would be five minutes of film!

Getting to see Peter every day made it all worthwhile, though, and she knew that he felt the same way about her. It was awful to think that the filming would soon be over, and Peter would be on his way to the West Coast. Still, she knew that they had a very special relationship, and would always be part of each other's lives. Peter had already told her that he'd be working on a movie in New York in March, and she'd be able to see him over spring break.

She smiled, thinking how much fun it would be to take him to some of her favorite places in Manhattan. There was that funny little place that had croissants on Lexington Avenue, and they could sip cappuccino in the Village. And Peter said the cast parties in New York were something else. She planned on going to every single one of them with him! It would be a miracle if they could crowd it all into two weeks. In the meantime, there would be letters and phone calls, of course, and Peter promised to call her the minute he got to L.A. . . .

"You look disgustingly cheerful for this hour of the morning," Pamela said in her husky voice. "It's inhuman to make people get up at the crack of dawn, and then expect them to remember lines! It's insane. Simply insane!" Pamela frowned at her over the rim of a steaming cup of coffee.

"Where did you get that?" Dana asked. "The catering truck isn't here yet."

Pamela licked her lips like a cat. "No, but the cafeteria is."

"I know that, but we're not supposed to leave the set," Dana protested. "Not for anything, they said."

"I didn't leave the set." Pamela laughed.

"Honestly, for a New Yorker, you don't seem to have much . . . imagination. I sent a nice little man to get me some. The one setting up the lights."

"He's the assistant director," Dana said, shocked.

"Bully for him." Pamela didn't say anything for a moment, and then said craftily, "Well, I guess I can stand anything for one more day. Even this rotten cold." She shivered and pulled her fleece-lined coat more tightly around her.

"What do you mean, 'one more day'?" Dana said absently. She was trying to keep an eye out for Peter, but couldn't spot him anywhere on the set.

"This is it. Fini. Like they say, the party's over." She stared at Dana. "Didn't you know the wrap party's tonight?"

"The wrap party?" Dana said.

"Surely you know what a wrap party is," Pamela said with heavy sarcasm.

"It's a party they have on the last day of shooting," Dana managed to say. Why hadn't Peter said anything to her? He must have known.

"Right. Go to the head of the class."

"But . . . it can't be over! They still have lots of crowd scenes to do. There's the fraternity party, and the scene in the forest. . . ."

"They decided to shoot them all out in L.A.," Pamela said airily. "They'd rather shoot everything on a backlot anyway. Location stuff always costs too much."

"But it won't look realistic," Dana protested.

Pamela laughed. "Well, who cares? This isn't exactly a film classic, is it? I hope you weren't expecting an award at the Cannes Film Festival."

Dana swallowed hard and didn't say anything. Maybe Peter hadn't known this was the last day of filming. That must be it! At least she could go to the wrap party with him. They needed to talk, to plan how they could see each other again. . . .

"That's your call," Pamela said, breaking into her thoughts again. "You're Susan, aren't you?"

"Yes," Dana said as the director lifted the megaphone again. Somehow she had to get through the day's filming, and keep her mind on her work. She'd manage to catch up with Peter before the wrap party. She just had to!

Meanwhile Faith had heard about the wrap party from an entirely different source — Alex. On an impulse, she had visited him again in the makeup tent, waiting for a moment when he wasn't busy.

"I want to show you something," she said shyly. She pulled out her portfolio and handed it to him.

"You did these?" he said, surprised. When she nodded, a big grin spread over his face.

"What do you think?" she said nervously. "I haven't shown them to many people. Just my roommates and my housemother."

He flipped through them slowly, giving each one his full attention. "I think they're marvelous," he said finally. "Absolutely marvelous. You've got real talent, Faith. A gift for seeing things as they are."

"You don't mind being included in the collection, then?"

"Of course not, I'm flattered. Who wouldn't be?" He paused and laughed. "Oh, wait a minute. I know someone who wouldn't be. You're not planning on bringing these to the wrap party tonight, I hope."

"The wrap party? You mean this is the last day of filming?"

"That it is. Tomorrow we fly out to sunny California." Some actors started drifting into the makeup tent, and he lowered his voice. "These are terrific, Faith," he said, handing her back the portfolio. "But if I were you, I'd keep them under lock and key. Be careful. These are too good to lose."

"I'll be careful," she promised. "And I'll see you tonight." Faith left the tent, and nearly bumped into Shelley who was standing outside.

"Here you are!" Shelley said. "I need to talk to you for a minute."

"Shelley, what are you doing here? I thought you were going to spend the whole morning going over your math problems."

"Something . . . something important came up," Shelley said falteringly.

"More important than your grades?" Faith said sharply. She really was running out of patience with her roommate. Shelley had promised to bring up her grades, and turn in the work she had missed. "If you're not careful, you're going to end up on academic probation, and maybe even get grounded. Just think about it!" Faith had more at stake than just concern for her friend, she admitted to herself. If Shelley was grounded, she'd make everybody in 407 absolutely miserable!

"Don't worry about that now," Shelley insisted. "Listen, let's go to the cafeteria and get some breakfast. I've simply got to talk to someone."

"Okay," Faith said. "But this better be good."

"You're not very hungry," Faith observed a few minutes later. Shelley wasn't even making a pretense of eating her French toast.

"I've got a lot on my mind," she said in a little voice.

Faith sighed and bit into a blueberry muffin. "Okay, spill it."

"I just found out that today is the last day of filming."

"Right. I just found that out, too. So what's the big deal?"

"That means the whole company is leaving tomorrow," Shelley went on.

"For sunny California." Faith looked at her. "Shelley, I've got the feeling I'm missing something, or you're leaving out a whole chunk of this story."

"Troy asked me to go with him." Shelley looked out the window as she said it, afraid to meet Faith's eyes.

"He what!" Faith exploded.

"He asked me to go with him," Shelley repeated slowly. "I haven't told anyone but you."

"I should hope not," Faith said. "They'd think you were nuts." Shelley's face clouded, and Faith went on in a softer voice, "This isn't a joke, right?"

"It's no joke. Troy asked me to go to L.A. with him to meet his agent, and then spend a few months in South America shooting a movie. He's sure he can get me a part," she said earnestly. "He's got the second lead. He plays this journalist who's on the trail of some treasure, and —"

Faith held up her hand. "Spare me the details." She paused, wondering what to say next. "Shelley, don't you understand? Troy is a . . . movie star. He's used to handing out lines. He'd tell you anything to . . . make an impression on you."

"He's not like that," Shelley said firmly. "He thinks I have real talent, and he wants to help me." She stood up and glared at Faith. "I should have known you wouldn't understand. No one does!" She turned and ran out of the cafeteria, leaving a very puzzled Faith alone at the table.

Should I tell Alison? she wondered. Shelley was in over her head, if she was really serious about going to L.A. with Troy Adams. But what could really happen? Shelley might be serious about it, but Troy obviously wasn't. Faith felt relieved. There wasn't a chance in the world that Shelley would be on that plane. But just to make sure, she'd keep her eye on her until the wrap party was over and Troy Adams was safely on his way to L.A. . . .

CHAPTER SIXTEEN

That evening, the scene in 407 was chaotic. "Sometimes this room seems too small for three people," Dana complained, as she and Faith bumped into each other on their way to the closet. Dana reached for a shimmery silk blouse her mother had sent her from New York, and slipped it over her head.

"We need more mirrors, that's for sure," Shelley said. She peered at herself and said nervously, "What do you think? Is it too boring?" She had changed her clothes three times and had finally settled on a pair of black pants and a white off-the-shoulder sweater.

"No, it looks great with your blonde hair," Dana told her.

"It's perfect," Faith agreed. She looked at Dana. "We're all going to go to the wrap party together, aren't we?" She was determined to keep an eye on Shelley, and make sure she didn't do anything crazy.

"Sure," Dana said, surprised. "And unless

we leave for Addison right this minute, we're going to be late."

"Okay, go ahead, and I'll catch up with you," Faith said. "I just want to throw these new prints in my portfolio." She carefully slid her glossy black-and-whites between transparent plastic sheets, and clicked them into the notebook. It really was the best work she had ever done. She took a final glance in the mirror and switched out the light. If nothing else, the wrap party should be interesting, she thought. It wasn't until she was halfway down the stairs that she remembered she had left the portfolio lying in plain view of her bed.

"Faith, hurry up!" Dana yelled from the landing. Faith hesitated. Should she go back and move the portfolio? No, that was silly, she decided. No one was going to come into her room and swipe it!

The first person Dana spotted at the wrap party that night was Peter. "Peter! Over here!" she yelled across the room. The lounge was packed with people and she was afraid he hadn't heard her. Then he turned and her heart sank when she realized that he had a girl with him. But who? Suddenly the crowd shifted and she recognized a familiar blonde head. Pamela.

It was too late to back down, and she forced herself to walk over to them. When she got closer, she saw that Peter had his arm lightly around Pamela's waist.

If Peter was embarrassed, he certainly didn't show it. "Hi, Dana," he said casually. "They've got some great food over there." He motioned to the long metal tables set up against the wall.

"Yes, why don't you help yourself?" Pamela added sweetly. She gave Dana a gloating smile.

"I'm not hungry," Dana said flatly. When was he going to get rid of Pamela? Apparently never! Even though he had dropped his arm from her waist, Pamela was standing very close, almost pressing against him, but Peter didn't seem to mind it one bit. She was searching her mind for something really biting to say when the director, Tony Albritton, joined them and started talking to Pamela. "There's some great music going to waste," Dana said lightly. Someone had brought a stereo system into the lounge and the sound of Duran Duran filled the room.

"I just finished dancing with Pamela," Peter explained. He smiled politely and turned his attention to his drink.

What was wrong with him? she wondered. He seemed like a totally different person. So cool and preoccupied, like a stranger. Pamela and Tony Albritton were still deep in conversation, and she decided to try again. "Want to wander around and meet some people?"

He shrugged, and looked a little uncomfortable. "Look, Dana," he began and then stopped.

"Yes?" she prompted him. She knew she wouldn't like what was coming.

"You're really a nice girl, but I think you should know that I'm here with Pamela."

"What do you mean you're here with Pamela! I've been waiting all day to see you! What about us?" She felt furious and hurt and humiliated, all at the same time. She didn't know it was possible to feel this rotten!

Peter swirled his drink around and looked like he wished he were someplace else. "Oh, come on, Dana," he said. "You and I are friends more than anything else. All fun and games, right? But Pamela — well, be reasonable, Dana. Just look at her." Dana dutifully followed his gaze to Pamela, who was laughing uproariously at something the director was saying. "She knows everybody in the movie business," he said softly. "Her mother has connections you wouldn't believe."

"But how will that help you?" Dana said, still puzzled. "You'll always have enough work, anyway. You said so yourself."

"Yeah, as a technician," he said derisively. "Do you think I want to lug cables around all my life? I want to be an actor, or maybe a director someday. And the Youngs are the ticket. Mother and daughter. In fact, Pamela was just saying —"

Dana didn't stick around to hear what Pamela had just said. She yanked on her coat, turned, and walked right out of Addison House. She couldn't believe it! Peter Marks

was a rat, a creep! She must have been out of
her mind to fall for him. The night was
piercingly cold, and a chill wind whipped
around her legs, but she barely felt it as she
hurried back to Baker House. She must have
been insane . . . yes, that was it, she decided.
Temporary insanity! She needed to talk to
someone. *Oh, Alison, please be there,* she
prayed silently as she raced up the stairs to
Alison's apartment.

Shelley noticed Dana's hasty disappearance,
but she had her own problems to contend
with. Where was Troy? She had made a big
circle of the lounge three times, and still
hadn't found him. He certainly wouldn't miss
a wrap party, would he? Anyway, she had to
see him and tell him she'd go to L.A. with
him. He must have fallen asleep, she decided
finally. There was no phone in the silver-
and-blue trailer, so she'd just have to go over
there and wake him up. He'd probably laugh
and thank her!

Shelley slipped out the back door of Addison and half-ran the distance to the trailer.
That's funny, she thought, when she got close.
There're lights on inside. She knocked hard
on the metal door for several minutes until
someone opened it. It was Troy, and he looked
puzzled.

"Hi, sleepy-head," she said to him. "You're
missing the party."

He blinked groggily as if he had never seen

her before. "What are you talking about?" he muttered.

"The wrap party. It's going on right now, in Addison House." She wondered why he didn't ask her in.

"Oh, the party," he said, rubbing his neck and stretching. "Well, I'll tell you, kid, I think I'll pass on it. You go ahead and have a good time, though." He made a motion to shut the door, but Shelley stopped him.

"Tomorrow," she pleaded. "What about tomorrow?"

Troy hesitated, and Shelley heard a burst of voices and laughter from inside the trailer. There was obviously a party inside. "Yeah, tomorrow, kid," Troy said quickly. "I'll see you tomorrow. It has to be in the morning, though. I fly out of here at noon." He flashed that famous smile one more time at her. "Have fun at the party!" And then he closed the door in her face.

For a minute, Shelley just stood there, too stunned to react. She wanted to cry, she wanted to throw something at him — she didn't know what she wanted! "I fly out of here at noon," he had said. Not a word about her. About them! Shelley's eyes stung with tears as she ran all the way back to Baker House. She couldn't go back to the wrap party, and she couldn't face being alone in 407. She needed desperately to talk to someone, and Alison was the best bet.

Dana was pouring out her soul to a sympathetic Alison when a tearful Shelley stood in the doorway. "This is the worst night of my life. Troy Adams is a rat!" she wailed. "A first-class rat!"

Alison smiled and waved her to a chair. "Sit down and join the club. Dana's just been filling me in on another world champion rat named Peter Marks. Shall we flip a coin to see which one is the bigger rat?"

"Troy Adams is," Shelley said flatly. "He said he'd make me a star, and take me to South America, and —"

"Take you to South America?" Dana said incredulously.

There was something about the way she said it that made Shelley forget she was supposed to be in the depths of despair. To her surprise, she felt herself smiling. "Yes," Shelley said, and started to giggle. "It sounds pretty crazy, doesn't it?"

"I have to admit it does," Dana told her and started to laugh.

"To make an adventure movie in the jungle!" she said. "With a trip up the Nile!" she added between bouts of laughter.

"The Nile's in Egypt, silly. I think you mean the Amazon," Dana laughed.

"That's it! The Amazon!" Shelley started to laugh all over again.

Alison stared at them in surprise. "Well, I've never seen anyone's mood change so quickly," she said with a smile. "Here I was all set to offer tea and sympathy, and it's turning into a party. Have some more cookies, gang, while I get the door. I have the feeling the Third Musketeer is here."

It was Faith, and she stopped in surprise when she saw Dana and Shelley sitting giggling in the middle of Alison's living room. "What's everybody doing here?" she demanded.

"We're having a summit conference," Dana said when she got her breath back. "Want to join in?"

"I've got a problem you wouldn't believe," Faith said, as Alison disappeared into the kitchen.

"After tonight, I'd believe anything," Shelley said, wiping her eyes.

"Okay, listen to this," Faith said. "My portfolio's gone. I decided to take some pictures at the wrap party, and when I went back to the room for my camera, I noticed it was . . . gone!"

"Gone?" Dana put down her cup and stared at her.

Faith shrugged. "Gone. Disappeared. Vanished. What else can I say? I left it on the bed, and —"

"And here it is," Alison said with a big grin on her face. "Everything is intact. I checked it." She handed Faith the portfolio.

"You found it?" Faith asked, jumping out of her chair.

"Let's say I rescued it." She smiled and curled up on a pillow. "When I was doing room check tonight, I spotted a certain person coming out of your room with it —"

"That certain person happened to be Pamela, I suppose," Faith said angrily.

Alison nodded. "I'm afraid so. I knew it wasn't the kind of thing you'd lend to someone — especially her — so I grabbed it for you."

"I saw her on our floor just as we were leaving for the wrap party," Shelley said. "She must have figured that was a good time to take it."

"Speaking of wrap parties," Alison said slowly, "is it safe to assume that *Midnight Whispers* is really wrapped up? That it's really out of everyone's system?"

"It's over for me," Dana said feelingly. "I've had enough of the movie business to last me a lifetime."

"Well, I had my brush with stardom," Shelley smiled. "Someday when I'm a grandmother I can tell my grandchildren that I had a hamburger with the famous Troy Adams."

"How about you, Faith?" Alison asked.

Faith was flipping through her portfolio and stopped long enough to grin. "I guess I'm the only one who doesn't have any complaints. I've got a start on a great portfolio." She paused. "It's too bad about the wrap party, though," she said. "We'll probably never have a chance to go to another one."

"Let's have our own wrap party right here," Alison suggested. "In fact, I'll even propose a toast." She lifted her mug of tea high in the air, and looked at the three girls. "To Foxfire Productions. May their movies be a big success."

"May they remember to send me my check," Dana said wryly.

"May they always remember Canby Hall," Faith offered, raising a cup of tea.

"And may they make their next movie someplace else!" Shelley added with a giggle.

"Amen to that," Alison said solemnly.